Keeping Humble

In God's Keeping

Book 3

By

Ronna M. Bacon

Micah 6:8. He has shown you, O man, what *is* good;
And what does the Lord require of you

But to do justly, To love mercy, And to walk humbly
with your God?

Philippians 2:3. Do nothing from selfishness or empty
conceit, but with humility of mind regard one another
as more important than yourselves;

NJKV

Table of Contents

Chapter 1

Struggling to keep his balance, Cayce Koyle plodded along a pathway, not knowing where it had started or where it would end. He stopped momentarily to wipe at his face, trying to clear away the sleet that was now falling, taking over from the flat fluffy snowflakes. Cayce looked around before his feet started moving again. He had no idea where he was or why he was out there. He stumbled and fell to his knees, the shock hitting him hard as it jarred his body. His head dropped for a moment before Cayce was on his feet, moving just in an effort to stay warm.

His face was burning with a fever that didn't abate. Cayce was sick and had no shelter that he could find and that he desperately needed. He had no idea why he was sick or even what day it was. It felt as if he had been searching on that pathway for weeks. He just had no concept of time.

Cayce paused once more, leaning against a nearby tree. He was shivering harder than he had been, the fever drawing him into a vortex of confusion and pain. The cold wind was driving through his heavy jacket and woollen toque and the gloves on his hands. His feet were freezing and starting to turn numb. Cayce could not see that far, his eyes only half open from how he was feeling.

Unable to move forward, Cayce just stood there. A hand was raised to rub at his dark brown eyes and then at his reddish blond hair. He was ready to collapse but he was aware enough that if he collapsed, he would not be able to pick himself up again. Cayce didn't even remember that his phone was not tucked into a jeans pocket. He just couldn't think, his mind was that foggy.

Haley Hagan raised her head from where she was crouching near a pile of sticks. She had been out collecting them for her woodworking projects. A sense that she was not alone surged through her. On her feet, Haley turned in a circle, her curiously coloured grey eyes without fear. Her russet curls blew in the wind across her face, causing her to grab at them to clear her vision.

Turning once more in a circle, Haley's attention was caught by the image of a figure standing nearby, leaning against a tree. Fear drove through her. She was normally fearless but today, she had felt as if she had been followed and that whoever it was, that person was still present. Picking up the bundle of twigs, Haley shrugged into her backpack and then walked cautiously forward, her eyes searching the area before she concentrated on the man standing there, not moving towards her. Haley began to pray for safety and protection, not feeling danger from the form in front of her but from someone watching and stalking her.

Haley stopped short of the man, frowning at him. Something was off with him.

"Hey, mister? Are you okay?" Haley waited for him to respond. When he didn't, she walked closer, a hand out to touch his face.

—

Cayce jumped at her touch. He thought that he was on his own but apparently, he wasn't. He squinted at the form in front of him, recognizing that it was a female.

"Are you okay?" The words seemed to echo in his brain before he shook his head, regretting it. "Here. Put your arm around my shoulders. We're not that far from my home." Haley reached for his arm, drawing it around her shoulders, and then wrapped an arm around him. She waited patiently for him to move. When he didn't, Haley nudged him forward gently.

Walking carefully on the icy path, Haley kept an eye on Cayce. She frowned at one point, recognizing him from church and a Bible study that she was sometimes able to attend. What was Cayce Koyle doing out here? And he was sick. That much she knew.

A yell from in front of her caused her to slip slightly, her arm tightening on Cayce to keep him upright. Her brother was moving towards her as quickly as he could.

"Haley? I thought that you were out looking for wood, not recovering men." Joshua paused for a moment. "Cayce Koyle? What's he doing out here?" He reached to help balance Cayce.

"I found him near Miller's pond. I don't know why he's out here. But he's sick, Josh, really sick. And this weather is not helping him." Haley bit at her lip, worried about Cayce and knowing that they needed to get him out of the elements and to warm and safety.

—

"We'll do that. Here, let me help him. You walk ahead of us." He handed her his walking stick. "Just be careful. The sleet has made this a nice icy walk." Josh grinned at his sister as she made a face at him. His attention then turned to Cayce. His thoughts were troubled as he carefully walked towards their home, his arm stronger than Haley's and more able to keep Cayce upright.

Ben Hagan looked around as he heard the door and then the shuffling sound of feet. He rose and walked towards his son and daughter, a frown on his face.

"Who do we have here?" He waited for one of the two to ask.

"Cayce Koyle. I found him out in the woods, Dad, but he's sick. Really sick." Haley was on the move to the spare room, pulling back the blankets and then almost running for Josh's room to gather some clothes. "Here, Josh. He'll need to warm up."

"Go ahead and get some broth or something hot for him, sis. I'll look after him." Josh looked at his father. "We're not going to be able to get him out of here to help."

Haley nodded and almost ran towards the kitchen, opening the fridge and then the freezer. She was desperate to find the broth and heat it, knowing that they needed to warm Cayce and do that carefully but quickly. Ben watched his daughter for a moment before he reached for the kettle and set it to heat before he looked for the hot water bottles.

10

"Dad? What do we do?" Haley's hands paused as she gripped the empty bottle.

"We get Cayce warm and treat him as best as we can." Ben had been a medic in the armed forces many years ago. "I'll see what I can do. If I need to, I can call someone for advice." He nodded at the broth. "Work on that." Ben gathered up the hot water bottles and stalked towards the bedroom.

Josh looked up as his father tapped at the door and then cracked it open. He had helped Cayce into a warm shower, dry clothes, and then into the bed. He helped his father tuck the hot water bottles around Cayce before he was into the bathroom and back with a cold cloth that he placed on Cayce's forehead. They needed to bring down his fever. Ben wasn't sure that these tricks would work but they needed to try. There was no way that they could make it into town, not with the sleet that was still falling and the iciness of the roads.

Josh walked towards the kitchen, hesitating as he watched his sister standing at the counter, her head bowed. She was praying, he knew, before he moved to stand beside her, an arm around her shoulders.

"How is he, Josh?" Haley's voice was barely audible.

"He's really sick, Haley. I can't tell you anything other than that. Dad will assess him and then decide from there what we can do." Josh walked over to peek out the window, unable to see out because of the ice covering it. "How long was he out there?"

"I don't know, Josh. You know how long I was." Haley turned to lean against the counter. She was troubled and puzzled at why Cayce was there. "I know of Cayce from church. Didn't his brothers just go through some horrible stuff?"

Josh grinned at her wording before he sobered. He was well aware that Arlyn and Briar, brothers of Cayce, had indeed gone through some rough stuff. The three men, triplets, were prominent in their town and their church. No one could explain totally why they had gone through what they had.

"They did. It's strange that they have all gone through something."

Haley frowned harder at her brother's wording.

"What do you mean, all three of them? We don't know that Cayce is going through anything."

"No, we don't, but God is nudging me that way. And I never ignore the nudges from God." Josh's words paused as a horrible thought shot through his mind. "And now you're involved with him."

Haley stared at him, her mouth open. She snapped it shut even as her head began to shake vigorously.

"No way, brother. There is no way that I'm going through anything like that. I don't know Cayce that well."

Josh was laughing at his sister even as Ben approached them.

"Neither did Skylor or Brynne and now they're happily married." Josh's hand went up. "It's okay, sis.

You found him and then we'll return him to his family as soon as we can get out safely. Dad?" Josh looked over at his father, frowning at the look on his father's face.

"It's okay, son. Cayce has settled for now but we'll need to watch him over the night." Ben reached for the teapot, pouring out a cup of tea and then standing to watch his two children. Something was about to happen, something dangerous and life-threatening, and that involved his beloved daughter. All he could do was pray for her.

Chapter 2

Early the next morning, Haley crept towards the bedroom where Cayce was fighting his fever and also for his life. He was dangerously ill and there was no way that he could be moved to a hospital. Ben had called his friend, desperate to have the physician come out. It was just not possible with the weather and the roads. Even though they lived just on the outskirts of town, only the main roads had been taken care of by that point.

Haley slipped into the room and then to her knees beside the bed. She reached for the cloth on Cayce's forehead, wringing it out in cold water again, and replacing it. Haley's arm slipped around his neck and raised it enough to get him to sip some water. Cayce let out a soft sigh although he was still feverish. His eyes opened up for a moment and then closed as he slept once more.

Rising to her feet, Haley stood for a moment, staring down at Cayce. She was puzzled as to why he was out in their woods, not that it mattered. They allowed people to use it for hiking but not for camping. But to find Cayce as he was, sick and delirious, out there had drawn her attention to the fact that maybe that wasn't such a good idea after all.

Returning to her bedroom, Haley snuggled back under her blankets. She began to pray for their house guest. Somehow, she had become involved in whatever it was that Cayce was deep into. Haley refreshed her memory of what she knew about the other two brothers of the set of triplets. She slept at last, not hearing the tap at her door a few hours later.

Josh opened his sister's bedroom door and then closed it softly. He knew that Haley had been up and tending to Cayce. He was heading that way himself to see what was needed. Josh was becoming worried about his sister. He had not idea what was going on. His sense was that Haley had become involved in an adventure that would bring danger to her.

Ben looked around at his son, worried about both of his children. It was not the first time that they had reached out to help someone. This time it was different. And he could not stop whatever was happening, no matter how much he wished for that and no matter how much he prayed for that.

"How is he, Josh?" Ben turned back to the frying pan on the wood stove, turning the bacon that he was frying.

"He's sleeping, I think, not unconscious. His fever seems to have come down some but not completely. I worry about him, Dad. His family must be looking for him." Josh reached for the plates of food that his father had dished up. "Haley is still sleeping."

"It's what she needs. She's been pushing herself far too hard lately. Being out there in the sleet storm yesterday hasn't helped." Ben sat at the table, his head bowing as he asked a blessing on their food.

"We need to reach out to his family." Josh turned slightly to stare towards the bedrooms. "They'll be worried about him."

"That they will. I'll call Ardan. I know him from the work committee at the church." Ben ate slowly, his thoughts troubled. "I want to know why Cayce was out here."

"It doesn't make sense. And he had been there for a while, I would hazard a guess." Josh was troubled as well. At a slight noise, he was on his feet, heading for Cayce. He found the other man sitting upright in the bed, a hand on his head. "Cayce?"

"Where am I? I need to go home. This isn't my home." Cayce began to struggle to free himself from the blankets, his strength not enough to unentangle himself.

"Lie back down, Cayce. You're too sick to go anywhere. Besides, the roads are impassable from here."

Cayce scowled at Josh. He didn't recognize him but didn't feel that Josh meant him any harm.

"I need to go. I'll walk." Cayce once more tried to rise but Josh's hand on his shoulder shoved him back down with just a light shove. "Why'd you do that?"

"You're too sick to go outside." Josh's grin lit his face. "Besides, Haley won't let you go."

"Who's Haley?" Cayce gave a low moan. "I hurt. My head hurts."

"Yeah, it will. You've been running a high fever and still are fighting it." Josh heard soft footsteps coming to a stop beside him. "Haley? Your friend here is trying to run away. You can't let him." His grin widened at the snort from his sister.

"My friend? Oh, no, he's just someone I found in the woods. Now, how is he feeling?" Haley's hand landed on Cayce's forehead, turning his attention to her.

Cayce stared up at the beautiful lady who stood near him. He thought that he knew her but he couldn't be sure. All he knew was that he didn't want her to go anywhere. That's what he was afraid would happen.

"You? Don't leave me. You found me. You can't desert me. I need your help. Someone is after me and I don't know who. Do you?" Cayce's eyes closed as he slept, leaving Haley staring at him in shock.

"Did he just say that?" Haley questioned her brother, a surprised tone in her voice.

"He did, sis." Josh could not control his chuckle despite the gravity of the scene. "I wonder what he meant."

"That he was being chased?" At Josh's nod, Haley shrugged. "I don't have any idea of what he was talking about." She turned away from the room, walking towards the front door, opening it to stare at the icy wonderland outside. There was no way that they could get Cayce home or even get one of his family members to them.

Ben wrapped an arm around his daughter's shoulders, praying for her. She leaned her head against her father, feeling the concern that he was feeling.

"Dad? Where do we go from here? Cayce just said that someone was after him." Haley was troubled, not sure if Cayce really was in danger.

"I suspect that's why he was out in the woods. It is strange that he was there." Ben stared out at the icy lawn. "And I am afraid that you have now become involved in that danger."

Haley drew in a deep breath. God had been talking with her and had told her that very fact. She trusted God enough that she knew He was in control. Haley just didn't have to like what she may well be facing.

Chapter 3

Two days later, Cayce laid back against the pillows stacked behind him. He stared around the room, not knowing where he was or who his host was. He could vaguely remember three different people bringing comfort to them, one a beautiful lady who he thought that he should remember. Only Cayce couldn't remember her. He could barely remember the last few weeks. He only knew that he was afraid and as on the run, but he couldn't remember why or from whom. Cayce still had not contacted his family. He didn't know where his phone was for one thing and for another he could vaguely remember threats directed at them.

Turning his head, Cayce looked towards the door as he heard soft footsteps. Haley appeared in the doorway, a tray in her hands that she set down on the bedside table. Her hand rested on Cayce's forehead, nodding as she did so. His fever was down, still not totally back to normal.

"How are you feeling today?" Haley watched him closely, seeing the whiteness of his face and the dark circles under his eyes.

Cayce shrugged, not sure what to say. He certainly wasn't himself.

"I'm sorry. I don't think that I know your name." Cayce waited for Haley to speak.

"I'm Haley Hagan. You're at our home, my Dad, Ben and my brother, Josh. I found you out in our woods on Saturday. You've been really sick." Haley found a chair to draw closer to the bed before she sat, not taking her eyes from Cayce. "Why were you out there?"

Cayce shrugged. He really didn't know why he was out there. He just felt a great fear as he tried to remember.

"I don't know, Haley, if I may call you that. I can't remember. I just know that I'm really scared. I don't scare easily." Cayce shifted on the bed, his head going down on the pillows. He yawned before his eyes closed and he slept.

Haley watched him for a moment before she was on her feet and setting her chair back along the way. She tucked the covers up closer around him before walking from the room and then to the basement where she had her workshop. Haley had found a niche for carved wooden crafts and had a list waiting for her to fulfill. She didn't feel like working on the craft but she had no choice.

A couple of hours later, Haley dropped the wood that she was working on, a groan coming from her. Someone was knocking at the door and she was on her own. She had been up and down the stairs over the hours, checking on Cayce.

Staring out of the window, a frown crossed Haley's face. She sighed as she reached for the door lock. Her father and brother were at work and she was on her own, other than for Cayce. And he certainly would be no help.

"Can I help you?" Haley winced as her voice sounded too loud.

"Oh, I'm sorry. I didn't expect to see you." Anna Koyle stood there. "I recognize you from church." She was hugging the younger lady, to Haley's surprise. "Now, where is that nephew of mine?"

Haley stared at her in amazement for a moment. She had not expected anyone to come out that day, certainly not one of Cayce's family.

"He's sleeping right now. He's been really sick." Haley bit at her lip before she continued. "Where's the rest of his family?"

"They are away at a conference. Cayce didn't want to go, he said. He had a stone that he had been working on." Anna wrapped an arm around Haley. "How be you take me to my nephew and then we'll talk."

Anna hesitated for a moment in the bedroom doorway, turning slightly to watch Haley walk away. She was troubled, she could tell. And that troubled Anna. Having had two of the triplets go through life and death adventures, she had prayed that Cayce would be spared. Somehow, she sensed that he was in the middle of an adventure.

Walking towards the bed, Anna stood beside it, staring down at her nephew. A hand rested on his hair, causing him to shift his head, his eyes flickering open and closed. A soft moan came from him before he was still.

—

Anna stood there for a few moments, praying for her nephew. She had no idea why he had been out here. Ardan had asked her to check in on him as they had already been out of town by the time Ben reached him.

Turning away, Anna made her way back to the kitchen, attempting to find Haley. Haley stood where she could watch Anna in turn, not comfortable being on her own.

"Anna?" Haley's voice had the lady turning towards her in an abrupt manner. "I'm sorry. I didn't mean to scare you."

"That's okay. I'm on edge, I think. This is not what I had thought to find." Anna turned to stare behind her. "How is he?"

"Cayce? He's better than he was but not out of the woods yet." Haley grinned as Anna laughed. "We still don't know why he was out here. I understand that someone named Joe is heading this way to speak with him."

"Joe? That would be correct. He'll speak with Cayce and then your family. I understand that you found him."

"I did. I was out there gathering branches for my craft business. I was in a rush because of the weather. I really thought I was seeing something when I saw him." Haley frowned as she thought about it.

"You found him out there?" Anna stared at the window. "And in the sleet? It's a wonder that he's as well as he is."

"It is. God has been gracious, Anna." Haley moved to pour them mugs of tea. "Dad should be home soon. Josh is away for a few days." Haley studied the older lady, seeing the concern that she was trying hard to hide. "Dad spoke with a friend of his who's a physician. Jack came out yesterday to assess Cayce and just told us to continue with what we were doing. He didn't think that he needed to be in the hospital. Besides, Dad was a medic in the armed forces and knew what to watch for."

"We cannot thank you enough, Haley, you and your family." Anna walked away, unable to control her emotions, heading back for her nephew. Her phone was out as she sent off a text message to her brother, just to let him know that she was with Cayce. Ardan was quick to reply, simply stating that he was praying for them both and that they would speak when Ardan and Bessie were back home again.

Haley followed Anna slowly, stopping just outside of the bedroom, watching Anna as she stood near her nephew. She sighed. She had no idea why Cayce had been out there or who was after him, but someone was. And she had become involved in it just because she was there. Haley frowned. She wondered why he was out there. He hadn't been able to say anything yet. Hearing a knock at the door, Haley headed that way, opening it to find a patrol officer standing there as well as the investigator. That must be Joe, Haley decided.

"Yes? Can I help you?" Haley's voice was low.

"Haley? We need to come in. I'll need to speak with Cayce." Joe was adamant on that, moving forward and entering the house. He nodded at the patrol officer who stepped back and stood outside of the door, his back to it.

Chapter 4

Cayce shifted restlessly as he awoke. He could hear a voice speaking with him before he squinted at the man sitting beside him. He knew the man but didn't know where he was.

"Joe? What are you doing here?" Cayce sipped at the glass of cold water that Joe held up to his mouth.

"Looking for you. I need to find out what you were doing out here. It's been about a week since you were last seen." Joe pulled up a chair and sat, knowing that it would take time for Cayce to remember and then speak about his adventure.

"Where am I? It's not home." Cayce looked around, squinting against the light.

"You are the Hagan's home. Haley found you and her brother helped bring you here. That was on Saturday." Joe sighed. This was going to be difficult, he could tell.

"They did. I need to find them." Cayce moved to shove the blankets back but didn't have the strength to move. "Where was I?"

"Where were you? When you were found?" Cayce nodded at Joe's question. "In the Hagan's woods. That was on Saturday in the middle of a sleet storm. That's why you're so sick."

"It was? I don't remember why I was out there. Do you know?" Cayce was struggling to remember.

His fever was still there, causing a headache that he was not sure that he would ever get rid of it.

"I don't know, Cayce. That's what I'm trying to determine and discover. I need you to remember anything that you can." Joe waited impatiently for Cayce to concentrate on him. That didn't seem to be happening. "Cayce? You need to talk to me."

Cayce sighed, his eyes closing for a moment. He prayed that he would remember but that didn't seem to be happening. He just didn't understand what had happened. Cayce knew that God was there and was leading in this adventure. He just didn't know where it was leading. Cayce was a humble man, not seeking out any praise for himself. He liked to stay in the background. That was not the case. Cayce was in the forefront and that disturbed him.

"Cayce?" Joe's voice broke into his thoughts, causing Cayce to turn towards him.

"I'm sorry, Joe. I don't have any idea what happened or where I was. I just can't remember. Where's my truck?"

"At your home. Your keys, wallet, and phone are sitting on your kitchen counter, just as you would have left them. The last time anyone spoke with you, we think, is when Arlyn called you on Wednesday morning. Do you remember that?"

Cayce shook his head, wincing as pain shot through it. He tried to think but that task just wasn't happening.

"No, I'm sorry, I don't. What does Arlyn say?"

"I haven't spoken with him yet. Your parents, Arlyn and Skylor, and Briar and Brynne are away at a conference. Do you remember that?" Joe's pen was posed over his notepad.

"No, I don't know that I do." Cayce caught sight of Haley heading their way, a tray in her hands. "Haley? You shouldn't be doing that. Let me." He tried once more to rise and again didn't have the strength to do so.

"It's fine, Cayce. Here, Joe, take this. If you need me, I'll be in the basement working. Your aunt has left, Cayce. She said that she'd be back either later tonight or tomorrow." She walked away, not seeing the look on Cayce's face as he watched her.

Joe had raised his head at that point after setting the tray down on a nearby table. He frowned and then sighed. Cayce was interested in Haley already and that would not be what he needed. Joe turned to study the door, thinking through what had happened.

"Cayce? What are you thinking?" Joe gave him a grin as Cayce's head shot around to face him.

"Why did you make me do that?" Cayce's eyes closed in pain. He didn't open them again, missing the look on Joe's face. When he did look up, he studied the light sage walls and cream trim. He liked those colours. Someone who was artistic had designed this room. "Joe, what do you know about Ben, Josh, and Haley?"

"What do I know about them? They are well thought of in the community. Haley in particular is well liked. She works behind the scenes, just like you

---

do. She has a humbleness about her that is not often seen but is just like you.”

Cayce was nodding. He was beginning to remember Haley and her family. He had always admired them, wanting to get to know them better. It appeared now that Cayce would be able to do that. Only he was very afraid for Haley, not knowing why. God was impressing on him that he would become involved in her life and she in his.

“What do you know?” Cayce turned back to Joe.

“Not a lot, Cayce. We’ve tried to track back your path but can’t do that. The weather covered your path and destroyed any evidence that may have been there. We’ve been through your home. Your aunt let us in. There is just nothing there that shows anything. It’s like you emptied your pockets and walked away.”

“Someone made me do that, didn’t they?” Cayce stared at Joe. “Who? Does anything show on the security feed?”

“We can’t access that without you or one of your family. Anna doesn’t have that access.” Joe reminded Cayce, a frown on his face.

“That’s true. I need to go there.” Cayce’s eyes closed as he slept, not realizing that Joe still needed to speak with him.

Joe stared at Cayce for a moment. How did he sleep so suddenly? Joe needed to talk with him and warn him that there was word on the street that Cayce was in danger although it would appear that Cayce was already aware of that.

———

On his feet, Joe searched for Haley, not finding her. He sighed once more, something he seemed to be doing with regularity. He walked out to his vehicle, standing for a moment and staring around. Joe felt very uncomfortable at leaving Cayce but he had no choice. He didn't see Haley standing in the open doorway watching him before she shut and locked the door and then headed towards where Cayce was sleeping.

Chapter 5

Haley shoved away the kitchen counter late that afternoon. She needed to be working on her crafts but had no interest in it at the moment. Walking through the house, Haley paused at her bedroom before she walked in and closed the door after her. She reached for her Bible, needing to find the peace and comfort from God that had been missing for the last few days. Her family would be home soon and ready for the stew that she had in the crock pot on the counter. Fresh bread sat on top of the overturned loaf tins.

Cayce turned slowly from where he had placed the folded night clothes that he had been provided on the bed. He had straightened up the covers before he had dressed, his motions slow and measured. His headache was still there but he had to accept that. God was there, Cayce was sure. He just didn't understand what had happened to him.

Walking through the house, a house that he didn't know, Cayce paused at the back door. His jacket hang there on a hook. He reached for it, found his toque and gloves, and shoved his feet into his boots. Opening the door, Cayce walked out of the house and away from it, his mind telling him not to but his thoughts were too foggy for him to listen to. He just kept walking, not realizing the consternation and fear that he would leave in his wake.

Josh walked into the house a couple of hours later, searching for his sister. He stood for a moment, watching her before he strode towards her and removed the carving tool from her hand. Haley stared up at him in shock.

"Josh? Is it that late already? Supper's ready." Haley shoved back her chair, ready to rise, prevented from doing that by her brother's hand on her shoulder.

"It's okay, Haley. We'll eat when Dad gets home. He said he'd be about an hour." His finger came out to touch the little beaver that she had been carving. "This is so lifelike."

Haley glowed at the praise from her brother. It was not the first time that he had done that but each time, it confirmed that she was doing what she loved and did best.

"Thank you. How was your day?" Haley listened carefully as Josh spoke, his voice happy as he described the tile design that he had been working on. He was a tile setter and loved working with the various tiles that came his way.

"How's Cayce?" Josh turned his sister towards the stairs to the main floor.

"He was sleeping when Joe left a few hours ago. I haven't heard anything from him in a while." Haley quickly ran up the stairs and towards the bedroom. She slid to a halt, seeing the bed had been made, the night clothes carefully folded and left on the bed, and no sight of Cayce. She spun to search for him, not finding him.

Josh had followed her and then began his own search. His hand paused as he reached for the coat hooks. Cayce's jacket was missing. Josh's eyes

—

dropped to the boot trays and saw that the other man's boots were missing. He reached for his own jacket, shrugging into it and then shoving his feet into his boots. He was out of the back door, searching for Cayce and not finding him.

Haley ran towards Josh as he stood at the edge of the driveway and the street that ran in front of their home. There had been no sign of Cayce. That worried and frustrated Josh.

"Josh? Where is he?" Haley slid to a halt, her hand reaching for her brother's arm to keep her balance.

"I don't know, Haley. I really don't know. I have no idea when he walked away. Do you?" Josh turned his head slightly to watch his sister's face, a frown on his face. There was something going on with his sister, and he was suddenly afraid for her. "When did you see Cayce last?"

Haley shrugged. She wasn't really sure what time that was.

"Joe was here. I checked on Cayce after that and he was asleep. I checked on our meal and then headed for my work shop." Haley was feeling very guilty. "I should have checked on him more."

"Not your fault, sis. You checked on him. He was sleeping. How were you to know that he would wake up and leave?" Josh frowned at the ground. "There's been a vehicle stop here."

Haley nodded, moving to one side as their father's vehicle approached and made his turn towards

---

the house. Ben parked and then walked back to his children.

"You two are out here for a reason. What is it?" Ben shifted his gaze between the two.

"Cayce has disappeared some time over the afternoon. Sometime after Joe left." Haley walked away from her male relatives, her phone out. She sent off a quick text to Anna and then to Joe. Both responded with dismay.

Joe set his phone back on his kitchen counter. He was off duty now, being told to take the next few days. He sighed. That wasn't about to happen. Joe reached for his phone again, calling in the missing Cayce before he reached to shut off the oven and then reached for his jacket and boots. He was heading back for the house where he had walked away from Cayce. He had not expected Cayce to disappear again. Joe reached out to Anna, asking her if she had seen Cayce. A surprised no sounded in his ear before he simply stated that Cayce was missing again.

Anna stared at the phone before she spun to grab her winter outerwear and then ran for her car. Heading for Cayce's home, she prayed for her nephew. The family didn't need Cayce disappearing again, not after what the other two had gone through.

Standing in Cayce's office, Anna drew in a deep breath. Cayce was not there, not that she had been expecting him to be. He was just not where they could find him. Anna sent off a text message to Joe before she slowly walked back through the home, trying to decide what was off about the house. Something was

---

and she sensed it. Anna just could not decide just what it was.

Joe drove slowly along the street towards the Hagan house. He was searching for any sign of Cayce but there was none. That worried and frustrated him as well. Where was he? All he could do was pray for God to protect him and bring him home to his family. Joe's thoughts turned to Haley as he wondered what kind of danger that she was now in. He was certain that she was, just having reached out to rescue Cayce.

Chapter 6

Haley stood at the end of the driveway the next morning. She was searching for any sign of Cayce and couldn't find one. She was praying for her new friend, knowing that was what she could do and probably at the time the only thing that she could do.

A vehicle coming to a halt startled her and Haley spun to face the men walking towards her. Fear sent her feet running towards the home. She just didn't make it in time. Haley was tackled and sent to the ground, the gravel scraping at her hands and face. She screamed for help before a hand was wrapped around her mouth as she was yanked harshly to her feet.

Shoved towards the vehicle, Haley fought the men to escape to no avail. A pair of handcuffs were snapped around her wrists and a dirty piece of cloth around her mouth. Shoved into the vehicle, Haley had no opportunity to shove open the opposite door and escape. A hard grasped her arm in a tight manner that let her know escaping wasn't an option. Haley began to beg God to free her and that prayer didn't seem to be working at the present time.

Haley screamed again as a blindfold was abruptly covered her eyes, preventing her from seeing where they were heading. She felt the vehicle accelerate quickly and then felt the shifting of the vehicles as corners were taken in a fast manner, sending her multiple times against the door. Haley was terrified. She had no enemies, not that she knew of, and this situation was not something that she had ever expected to find herself in.

The vehicle came to a dead stop near a building, the driver exiting and heading for the door. He stepped through into the building and then returned, nodding at the man sitting beside Haley. Haley was pulled roughly from the vehicle, fighting as best as she could to escape. That just didn't happen. She was bundled roughly into the building and then down a hallway where their footsteps echoed in the emptiness. Shoved just as roughly into a room, Haley hit her hands and knees, the jar sending pain through her whole body.

The man stood over her before a hand reached out and hauled her to her feet, sending her to a sitting position in a chair. The hand cuffs were unlocked from one wrist and then locked around the chair rung behind her back. Haley struggled to escape once her hand was free but that didn't happen either. She just could not escape from the man.

Footsteps sounded as the man walked away, leaving her in darkness. She reached for her blindfold and gag, removing them. She was in darkness, with no light at all. Haley could not move from the chair, it was impossible to do that.

Hours seemed to pass but afterwards she found out that it had only been an hour. The blackness had driven her into herself and the only comfort that she had was to pray. And even then, Haley felt as if her prayers were not going anywhere.

Haley stood, walking around to the back of the chair. Feeling at the rung in the dark, she nodded. It was very thin and felt very brittle. She tugged at the hand cuff and felt the wood moving. Kneeling, she placed one foot on the rung and then wrapped a hand on the cuff and began to pull at it. She finally heard a crack and stopped working at the rung. Haley looked around, listening for anyone who might be coming back into the room.

Finally freeing the cuff from the rung, Haley shoved aside the splinters of wood. She was on her feet, an ear pressed to the door, listening for anyone who might be outside. Haley drew in a deep breath and reached for the door knob that she could feel in the darkness. She twisted it, surprised to find it unlocked and the door opening. Haley crept through it, her eyes briefly closing against the light that shone into them. She squinted against the light before she shrugged. There didn't seem to be anyone in the area but she could hear subtle movements. Walking towards the sound, Haley kept her eyes moving, her head turning as she moved through the debris on the floor. She set her feet carefully down so that she did not make any nose.

Haley paused frequently, her head turning constantly to search for anyone who might mean her harm. There was no one that she could see, but she seemed to feel as if there was someone watching her from somewhere. Haley continued to search, sensing that Cayce was in the same building.

Hesitating at a door, Haley bent her head and began to beg God that Cayce would be in there and that he would be okay. She reached a hand out to place flat on the door and then shoved at it. The door creaked open as she waved at the dust and cobwebs that floated into her face. Haley stepped into the room, blinking rapidly as she did so. She searched the room, a sound coming from her before she was running towards the figure huddled in a chair. A hand rested on the man before it was under his chin, raising his head.

Cayce roused somewhat as he felt a gentle hand on his face and then a female voice talking to him. He couldn't understand the words, though. He was in a fog of pain and fever and had no idea who the lady was unless it was one of his brothers' wives. But why they would be there, he didn't know. In fact, Cayce had no idea where he was.

Haley wrapped an arm around Cayce, looking around again. It was strange, she decided, that he was here in an unlocked room. He could just walk out if he really wanted to. She pulled him to his feet, her arm tightening around him, and then led him carefully to the door. Haley peeked out into the hallway, trying to decide which way to go. She turned to her left, her arm around Cayce persuading him to walk that way.

Cayce stumbled slightly as he walked forward, his arm around Haley. He blinked down at her, thinking that he should know her but he didn't or couldn't remember her name. The couple reached the outside door, with Haley hesitating once more before her hand landed on the door and she shoved at it.

The sun shone down on them as they stepped carefully out into the snow that had fallen. Their footsteps showed plainly where they were heading. Haley was worried about that but there really wasn't anything that she could do about it.

—

Haley shifted her hold on Cayce, stopping him for a moment as she studied the area. She had no idea where exactly they were except that they were in a run-down area of town. Or so she thought. Walking forward once more, Haley stumbled slightly and felt Cayce's arm tighten on her.

Cayce stopped walking forward, his face raising to the sun. He knew that he was sick and thought he was delirious. There was no way that he would be walking with a lady with an arm around her. He didn't date, not ever, yet here he was.

"Cayce? Are you okay?" Haley's voice finally broke through the stillness.

"Who are you? And no, I don't know that I am okay." Cayce stiffened his knees, feeling as if he would just collapse .

"I'm Haley. You've been sick and staying with my father, brother, and myself. You disappeared and then I disappeared. You need to be somewhere safe where you can get treatment." Haley was beginning to worry greatly about Cayce.

Cayce shrugged and then started walking again, not sure where he was heading. Haley sighed and walked with him, searching once more for anyone watching for them or for anywhere that she could find help.

Chapter 7

Arlyn and Briar stood in their brother's home, staring at their father. The three men had come to that home, praying that Cayce would be there. Unfortunately, he wasn't. They had searched his home, the garage, and then the workshop where he did his soapstone carving.

"Where is he?" Arlyn spun in a circle, not sure where to go or where to look.

"I have no idea, son." Ardan was distraught that his other son was going through this as had his brothers. "I spoke with Ben and he has no idea where he is. And now Haley has gone missing."

"Haley? She's missing? When?" Briar rubbed at his cheek, disturbed at that thought.

"This morning. They have no idea what happened. She was home alone and working on her crafts and then just wasn't there when Josh came home for lunch." Ardan paced away from his sons, his phone out to call Joe. That call went to voice mail, which frustrated Ardan.

Briar walked back out of the house, searching around the yard before he stood on the city sidewalk, not sure where he needed to be. He frowned as he watched a couple walking towards him, arms around one another. Briar stared harder before he gave a shout and began to run for the two people. He slid to a halt, a hand out to stop them.

"Cayce? What are you doing here? Where were you?" Briar's words bit at Cayce.

Cayce paused, his head raising. He stared at Briar, not sure who he was.

"Who are you?" Cayce's voice was barely audible.

"I'm your brother. Briar. Where have you been?" Briar reached an arm around Cayce, helping to take his brother's weight from Haley. She stared around Cayce at him, a frown on her face.

"Briar? I don't remember. Do you know where I was?" Cayce stumbled slightly as he walked towards his house. He didn't see Ardan and Arlyn waiting for him, frowns on their faces.

Ardan reached for Haley, gently moving her away from Cayce despite her protests. Arlyn moved in on the other side of Cayce, helping his brother into his house and then to his bedroom, despite his protests.

Cayce stumbled through the house thirty minutes later. He had showered, shaved, and dressed in clean clothes, feeling a bit more like himself. He was on a search, looking for the lady who had helped him.

Haley turned from where she had been staring out of the kitchen window, eyeing Cayce for a moment. She frowned as she saw the vulnerable and lost look in his eyes. She didn't think that he was like that. Haley knew from what her brother had said that Cayce mentored young men and teenagers but gave all the glory to God for his ability to reach them. He took no credit for himself. Haley knew it was the same for

---

his carvings. He had worked as a zoologist before his art took off and he had resigned to spend the time doing what he loved best.

"Cayce?" Haley stood where she was, not sure if she should approach him. Anna and Bessie had appeared with clean clothes for her as well, courtesy of one of the young wives. Haley had been grateful for that but more grateful when Briar had found a hacksaw and taken off the hand cuff that had been dangling from a wrist.

"Haley? Please don't leave me. I can't do it if you do." Cayce was across the room, wrapping her into a tight hug. His chin rested on the top of her head as his eyes closed. He was fighting his emotions, ready to weep but not wanting to weep in front of this beautiful lady.

Haley was shocked at Cayce's actions but more so at his words. What did he mean? She had no clue. They were basically strangers. Seeing movement in the hallway, Haley peered around Cayce. He was just refusing to let go of her.

Joe stood and watched the couple, a frown on his face. This was not Cayce to hug a lady like that. He had heard Cayce's broken words and frowned deeply. His eyes locked with those of Haley, seeing the questions that she would not ask.

"Cayce?" Joe stepped into the kitchen, his footsteps and voice causing Cayce to jump and then spin, keeping an arm around Haley. "We need to talk."

"We do?" Cayce sighed, reaching for a chair and sitting. He still felt feverish and weak. His hand reached for Haley's to draw her down to a chair beside him. "Haley can't leave. She needs to stay with me." Cayce had no idea why he was saying that. He couldn't remember if he had been told that or if Haley had been threatened. Cayce needed to remember that. Something was driving him to try and protect her. He just didn't know why or who had threatened her. But something was telling him that she had indeed been threatened.

"I'll allow it this once, Cayce." Joe reached to pour them all mugs of coffee and then sat, his notepad out in front of him, his phone set to video to capture what Cayce had to say. Then his gaze turned to Haley, watching her watch Cayce. Something was going on there, Joe decided. He just didn't know what. Joe's gaze shifted to Cayce. He had no idea what his friend was thinking. Cayce's face was blank. It was usually animated.

"Joe? Where were we?" Cayce looked up at his friend, not sure what to ask or to say.

"We don't know, Cayce. We haven't been able to trace your path. Do you know where you were?" Joe's pen was posed to take his notes.

Cayce shook his head. He had no idea where they had been. He shared a look with Haley who simply shook her head. She had no idea where they had been. They had walked until she found a street that she recognized and then headed for Cayce's home. It had been a long walk, that much Haley knew.

"I'm don't know what happened, Joe. I'm sorry. I was too out of it to know that I was kidnapped again.

—

I roused when Haley found me and then walked us to here." Cayce's head went down on his folded arms and he slept.

"Did he really just do that?" Joe shared an incredulous look with Haley. "Haley? What can you tell me?"

"What can I tell you? I was just out looking around the driveway for any sign of anything to show what happened to Cayce. A car drove up, men jumped out, and shoved me inside. I was handcuffed and had a blindfold and gag slapped on my face. Then I was handcuffed to a rickety old chair in a room. I was able to break a rung of the chair and then searched the building. I found Cayce, roused him enough to get him on his feet, and then walked us here." Haley was angry. Her head turned as she heard familiar voices and was on her feet, almost running for her father and brother.

Ben wrapped his daughter tight in his arms, having feared that he had lost her for good. Josh stood with a hand on his father's shoulder and the other one on his sister's back. Tears sparkled on his face for a moment as he thanked God for bringing the couple home. Josh just didn't know what to expect in the future but he feared for his sister and their new friend.

Chapter 8

Ben turned as he felt a hand rest briefly on his shoulder. Ardan stood beside him before he pointed to the back yard. The two fathers walked outside, both distressed at what had happened to their children.

"Does Cayce remember anything?" Ben broke the silence between them at last.

"No, he doesn't. He has no idea what happened to him. All I know is that he is deeply worried about Haley. Cayce seems to think that he was looking for her that day she found him in the woods. He just doesn't remember why. All I know is that Cayce is really worried about her." Ardan rubbed at the back of his neck. This was not Cayce to be like this, not about a lady. He had worried about his brothers' wives but he had never worried about a lady in quite this way before.

"Is that what he says? It's strange, Ardan. Haley should not have been out there that day. I asked her not to, seeing the weather report. I was doing some work in my office and when I came back out to the main rooms, she was gone. Josh took off after her once the weather started to change and he got home from work." Ben sighed. "This is strange, Ardan. Your three sons are going through stuff that no one ever should."

"No, they shouldn't. But it happens. We have friends who have gone through stuff like this, even to the point of almost dying. I suspect that they'll be looking into all this and passing their findings on to both the boys and Joe." Ardan turned to face the house. "I also suspect that Cayce is not wanting to let Haley out of his sight."

"That's what we all think. But it can't happen. Haley needs to go home and do her work. She has pending orders that are piling up and needs to address that." Ben sighed, a deep sigh that seemed to come from his very toes. "God is here, Ardan, and in control. It's hard to see that and accept it. Your son is humble about his work and what he does with his spare time. All the glory goes to God."

"That described Cayce so well. He doesn't want any praise for what he does. This is why this is so odd for him. He doesn't seek out any limelight but has with Haley. God has brought them together. She should not have been out there that day. Nor should he. I just wish he could remember where he was and how long he was out in the open." Ardan looked up at Arlyn and Briar who had approached them. "Boys?"

"It's okay, Dad. Cayce is sleeping again, this time in the kitchen. We tried to get him to go and lie down on his bed. He is refusing to. He wants or rather needs to be need Haley. She'll be going home soon. How do we do this?" Arlyn was worried about his brother. He could not stay overnight as much as he wanted to. He and Skylor were due at a meeting in a short while and needed to leave.

"I don't know, son. You two need to leave. I'll stay for a while. I know Mom is wanting to stay as is Anna." Ardan hugged his sons and their wives and sent them on their way. He then turned back to Ben, finding Josh beside his father. "Fellows?"

"We're heading home, Ardan. We need to get Haley home as much as she is digging in her heels not to leave. She wants to talk with Cayce again about what happened. Joe hasn't been able to find out much from her. She either doesn't know or isn't saying." Josh gave a grim smile. "And I would hazard it is that she doesn't want to say."

Ben nodded. Josh knew his sister only too well. Haley would refuse to say anything if she wasn't sure of something or if it meant harm to someone else. And she was uncertain, Ben knew, as to what Cayce was facing or who was after him. Haley thought through everything deeply before she would speak, if she even did speak.

Haley walked towards the men, her arms wrapped around her abdomen. She didn't want to to go home but she didn't have any choice. Joe had tried to get her to remember more than what she had said. Haley had just shaken her head and walked away. Joe had stared at her and then left, needing to be elsewhere.

Ben wrapped an arm around his daughter, distraught at what she had gone through. He knew that it wasn't over, not yet, and that she would likely find her life becoming more difficult and more dangerous. He prayed for his daughter and then for Cayce. Ben's eyes shifted to Josh, finding his son watching his sister closely. There was a close bond between the two, more than he had seen between other families, other than the Koyles. He sighed once more before turning Haley towards his truck, tucking her into the front passenger seat. Josh hesitated for a moment before he slid into the back seat, the door shutting out the cold air and the

<hr>

stillness. He was confident that something else was about to happen and that they had no control over that. Josh's attention turned to his sister, watching her as his father drove back towards their home. She was not speaking, remaining still in the seat. This was not Haley. She would have been discussing this in the past and shifting on her seat. Whatever had happened to her or had been said to her had stopped that.

Briar walked backed into Cayce's home, searching for his brother. He stood for a moment before his hand was around Cayce's arm, waking him up and then making him move to his bedroom. He tucked the blankets around Cayce, a hand resting on his brother's shoulder as he prayed for him.

Arlyn was in the hallway, watching, praying for his brother as well. He backed away as Briar approached him. He could hear their wives in the kitchen with Bessie. Where their father was, they weren't sure. He had been around and then disappeared.

"Briar?"

"He barely roused when I made him come from the kitchen. I don't know, Arlyn. I really don't know what happened to him. I wish we could figure it out but we just don't have enough information. Joe is at a loss. Without knowing what happened to start it all off, he can't figure it out. We've checked his security feed and didn't see anything off about it. That makes me wonder if the security feed was tampered with." Briar stared down the hallway, not sure what to think or say.

—

"That's what Dad asked. I put in a call to Blackie and asked if he or Simon could take a look at it. They'll be around tomorrow." Arlyn paused, a thought crossing his mind. "We need to have them bring Julia and Eavan with them. They need to share their stories with Haley."

"And Haley needs to hear them." Briar sighed once more. "This is so hard, you know. We went through this and prayed that Cayce would not. That's not how God is allowing life to happen. I am confident that God is here and in control. It just hurts to have to see one more of us face something."

"It is. And God has walked this path before Cayce and Haley." Arlyn gave a half smile. "Haley really didn't want to leave."

"No, she didn't." Briar studied his mother as she approached them. "Mom?"

"Cayce? Is he sleeping?" She hugged her two sons before moving past them to stand in the bedroom doorway. "He's hurting, boys, and there is nothing that we can do to relieve his worry."

Chapter 9

Haley stared down at the little beaver that she was carving from a piece of wood. Her hands were working away automatically while her mind was deep into the mystery that she had found herself involved in. Haley worried about Cayce, not having spoken with him that day. She had not wanted to walk away from him the day before but she had had no choice.

Josh had found her earlier that morning, just to give her a hug and pray for her. He was highly worried about her, just now knowing why or where the danger was coming from. He had stood for a moment before praying for her and then walking away. Josh had shaken his head at his father before both men headed out for the day.

On her feet, Haley reached for the orders that she had printed, sorting through them to find what she had on hand to fulfill them. Hours later, she stood at the back of her car, a hand on the trunk to shut it. Haley shivered, spinning in a circle. Someone was out there and that someone meant her harm. Her hand rested on the phone in her jacket pocket before she ran for her car door, diving inside and locking it behind her. Haley's hand was shaking almost too much to turn the key in the ignition. She took off almost too fast, the car swerving from side to side on the road as she sped away from her driveway.

Finished at the post office, Haley stood on the sidewalk, wanting to go home but too afraid to do so. Instead, she slipped into her car and pulled away from

---

the curb, heading for Cayce. She just prayed that he was up and ready to talk with her.

Cayce looked up from his work. He had brought what he needed to the kitchen and had been working there. He was too afraid to work in his shop, not quite knowing why but he suspected that was where he had been when he disappeared. From what his brothers told him, Cayce had been missing for about three days when he stumbled through the woods and was found by Haley.

Hearing the doorbell, Cayce hesitated to head that way. He only felt fear and that was not him. Praying for peace and courage, Cayce crept towards the front door, stretching to look out the side window without being seen. He frowned. The lady he had just been praying for was standing outside his door. He unlocked it, finding Haley turning to face him. Cayce didn't think, simply opened his arms and found Haley almost running to him to be hugged tightly by him.

Haley hugged Cayce, not wanting to let go of him. She was terrified, she had to admit to herself. Cayce made her feel safe. That and the fact that she had to trust God to protect them both. Haley had no idea what was happening, only that they were in danger.

Cayce backed away from the door far enough to be able to shut it and then reach to lock it. He was feeling unsafe that morning. Every time he stepped outside of the door into the yard, Cayce felt as if he was being spied on. He had walked the yard all the while speaking with Joe on the phone. Joe had called, just asking how Cayce was and if he could remember

—

anything at all. Cayce had answered in the negative. He had no idea who had abducted him, if that was what had happened nor why. He was an artist and his work could not be used for anything other than what it was. Now, if he had still been a zoologist, Cayce could see someone going after him.

Haley shoved away from Cayce to stand back and stare at him. She had no idea why she had come to find him. Cayce stared back at her, not sure why she had suddenly appeared. He was glad, though, that she had. Cayce wanted to protect her and couldn't when she was away from him. Once more, he tried had to remember why he felt that way and couldn't.

"Cayce? Who is doing this to us? And just where did you come from that day?" Haley was deeply troubled that Cayce had been wandering out in the sleet storm. If she had not been out there that day, he may well have died.

"I don't know, Haley. I just don't know. All I know is that I have to protect you and I don't know how to do that." Cayce's hands clasped together on the top of his head. "How do we find out?" Cayce wrapped an arm around Haley and directed her to the kitchen. "I've been working in here. I don't feel safe in the work shop right now."

"That's where you were taken from, isn't it?" Haley was confident in her words. "How do we find out who?" She reached for Cayce's mug and refreshed his coffee before pouring herself one. She turned to lean against the kitchen counter, looking around at the two-tone green cabinetry, the white back splash and the pale yellow walls. "I like your kitchen."

—

52

Cayce looked at her in surprise. He then looked around the kitchen.

"I have just repainted it. I needed something different. It felt dated beforehand." Cayce waited for Haley to sit before he sat down in the chair in front of his work. He picked up a carving tool, losing himself in his work. Cayce forgot that Haley was there, concentrating on the soapstone.

Haley watched him for a while before she was on her feet, wandering through the house. She liked the colours that he had chosen to paint the rooms. It was a house that she could live in, she decided, uncertain as to why she felt that way. Haley stopped in Cayce's office, not feeling as if she was intruding in his home.

Cayce looked up two hours later, surprised to see how much time had passed. He looked for Haley to still be sitting there but she wasn't. On his feet, Cayce almost ran through his house, looking for her. He paused in the doorway to the office, finding Haley seated on the loveseat there, a book in her hand. She looked up as she heard him, a frightened look crossing her face.

Sitting beside her, Cayce studied her, seeing a look in her eyes that gave him hope that she was willing to go along with what he wanted to ask. He felt driven to protect her. Cayce just didn't know why.

"How do I protect you, Haley? I need to do that." Cayce stared at Haley, his eyes full of trouble and fear as well as a lost look that she had seen before. There was also a look of wistfulness and uncertainty there as well.

—

Haley studied him, not sure how to respond. She frowned at him, seeing the vulnerability in him once more.

"You're trying to do God's work for him, Cayce. He's in control and protecting me." Haley's hand reached for Cayce's hand, finding his fingers curling around hers.

"I know, Haley. He is in control, but you need someone here on earth to stand in front of you." Cayce sighed, not sure how to express what he wanted to say. "Marry me, Haley. Marry me and let me protect you." He didn't look at her. He didn't want to see her rejection of his proposal on her face.

Haley stared at him, her mouth opening and closing. She had vowed never to marry, not wanting to, but this? This was not how she ever dreamed of receiving a proposal. Haley had to admit that Cayce did fit the image of her dream groom. She just wasn't ready for this.

On her feet, Haley ran for the door and then was out of it and in her car driving away before Cayce could even follow her. He stood, hands dragging down his face, before he wrapped his arms around himself and then stared up at the darkening sky. He sighed. Cayce would need to find her but not that day. Haley needed some time. He turned and stopped in his tracks before he reached for the paper half hanging out of his mailbox. He studied it before he stepped back into the house and locked himself in.

Heading for the kitchen, Cayce studied the mess from his work and then just reached for a bowl and dished up the chili that his mother had started in his crock pot. He sat, bowed his head to pray, and then ate. Cayce was deeply troubled, eyeing the paper before he found his phone and sent off a text message to Joe.

Chapter 10

Joe stood in Cayce's kitchen an hour later. He took with thanks the meal handed to him, finding space at the table to set his bowl down and then eat. Joe had not been surprised to receive that call from Cayce. His hand reached for the folded piece of paper.

"Have you read this yet?" Joe looked up at Cayce.

"No, I haven't." Cayce sat with his arms folded on the table, his eyes on the tabletop. "I expected something like this, given what his brothers had gone through.

Joe nodded, knowing that Cayce was hiding from danger. Only, that never worked out well. Cayce needed to know what he was being threatened with.

"Have you remembered anything at all?" Joe waited patiently for Cayce to respond. Cayce was a deep thinker and sometimes it took time for him to respond to questions.

"Nothing at all, Joe. I can't remember leaving my shop or where I was. I really don't remember those days at Haley's family home or even disappearing again. I don't know who was responsible for what I went through or who took Haley captive. I just know that I need to protect her. The only thing is that I don't know why." Cayce looked up at that point. "How do I find out what happened?"

"We're working on that, Cayce. Unfortunately, we can't find out what happened. No one saw anything. Your video feed was tampered with. The piece that was tampered with has disappeared. How do we protect you?"

"I don't know, Joe. I don't know. I want to protect Haley. How do I do that?" Cayce shifted on his chair, the feeling of uncertainty once more flowing through him.

Joe studied his friend, knowing that Cayce was speaking from his heart. He was the quiet one of the triplets, but when he spoke, his words affected those around him.

"We'll work on that, Cayce. It may mean that we have to put you two somewhere together with a security team to watch you both." Joe finally rose, taking the paper with him. He had sealed it into an evidence bag. The wording on it was very vague, which is what he had expected.

Cayce paced his home, his phone in his hand. He was studying his message, praying that he would have one from Haley. Only there wasn't one. Cayce had reached out to Josh when she didn't respond to his message asking if she had made it home. Josh had replied that she had but how was Cayce? He had not known how to respond. He had no idea how he was to feel or what he was to think.

Haley looked around as she heard steps on the stairs. She had been unable to sleep and had instead headed for her work room and her orders. Ben appeared, his eyes thoughtful as he studied his daughter. Something had happened that day and he wanted to know what.

"Haley? What happened today?" Ben found a seat on a stool, an arm resting on the work table. He studied his daughter, seeing changes that he prayed were only temporary.

"Dad? What do I do?" Her voice trembled as she spoke. Haley set aside what she was carving and looked up at her father.

"What do you do? I'm not sure I know what you mean." Ben looked up as he saw feet resting on a step and knew that Josh had taken a seat on the stairs.

"About Cayce. He wants to protect me so much. He asked me to marry him so that he could." Tears sparkled in Haley's eyes. She was torn about what route she should take.

"He did, did he? And you think he's just doing it out of kindness?" Ben waited until Haley nodded. "You two have a connection now, love, that is not ordinary. It happened with his brothers and their wives. Cayce is a quiet man, a man of few words. I know that he is deeply troubled about how to protect you. We don't even know how to, not knowing what happened or who it was." Ben drew in a deep breath. "We will pray with you, Haley. I would suggest that you speak with Skylor and Brynne. They know to some degree what you are facing. And I know that it will get much more dangerous for you both. At some point, Joe may want to put you two somewhere safe with a security team to guard you. As a married couple, it would be easier." His hand went up at Haley's protest. "That is no reason to marry. Pray over what Cayce asked. Seek counsel including from our pastor. Talk to me or Josh. Only take that step if

—

58

God had impressed on you that it is His will to do that." Ben prayed for his daughter before he was on his feet to hug her. "Don't stay up too late, love." He walked away, his steps heavy as he climbed the stairs. Ben paused to lay a hand on his son's shoulder, knowing that Josh was also highly worried about his sister.

Ben sank into his easy chair, his head buried in his hands. This is when he needed his wife, Eve, to be with him, to counsel and console their daughter. Cancer had taken her far too soon from them, when his children were small. Ben had struggled to raise them, especially troubled about Haley. And now this with Haley? Ben had no idea what to expect or how to prevent any danger for his beloved daughter. And he had no idea what had started it with Cayce. No one seemed to know. And that was worrisome. If they didn't know, then they could not take precautions or even find the ones responsible.

Haley watched her father walk away from her, sighing to herself. She seemed to be so troubled but she had no idea how to solve whatever it was. On her feet, Haley paced, a hand rubbing at her cheek. Her thoughts were more than troubled and Haley knew that she would not sleep that night. She reached for her phone, scrolling through all of her messages, stopping at the one from Cayce. She gave a small smile and then responded. Haley had no idea why he would have included red hearts with his message. She had to pray over what he had asked and then seek counsel.

The ringing of the doorbell caused her to jump and then head towards it. She peeked out with a frown on her face before she opened it.

Skylor and Brynne stood there, not sure if they should have come but they had even the push from God to do so.

"Skylor? Brynne? What are you two doing here? Come in." Haley closed the door behind them before pointing towards the kitchen.

"We're here to pray with you and then see what we can discover. We'll stay for a while, if we may, unless you need to work?" Skylor was now hesitant that they were there. It had seemed like a good idea at the time.

"It's okay, Skylor." Haley squinted at the clock. "It's close enough to supper. Will you two stay? Dad and Josh are away tonight. So if you will, I would appreciate the company."

"We can. The guys are with Cayce, trying to work through all this. I don't know that we'll figure it out before you two are hurt." Brynne reached to help Haley dish up their plates of stew. "We need to stick together, Haley. We truly do."

Chapter 11

Haley stared down at her bowl of stew. She wasn't hungry but she knew that she had to eat. She listened to the quiet words between the two other ladies, wishing that she was a part of their group. Haley didn't have a lot of friends, being more into her work than into making friends and had always been that way.

Skylor looked over at Haley, seeing the wistful look on her face. Her hand reached to touch Haley's, causing that lady to jump.

"Haley? What can we do for you? How do we pray for you?" Skylor's voice was soft as she questioned Haley.

Haley shrugged, a sober look on her face, but her eyes hopeful.

"I don't know. I just wish this had never happened." Haley was sober as she spoke, despair in her voice. "I just want to know what happened to Cayce to bring him out here. He was far from home." Haley's head turned as she heard the sound of a vehicle, one that she didn't recognize. She was on her feet and headed for a window to peer out when the door crashed open. The splintered wood dropped heavily to the floor.

Haley screamed as she saw the men charging into her home and then tried to run for the other door, the other two ladies in front of her. She didn't make it in time. A hard hand grasped her hand and spun her around. Haley screamed even as she struggled to escape the hand, her own hands flying as she struck out in fear. The man's other hand became a fist and then slammed into Haley's face. Her body went limp, only held up by the grip that the man had on her arm.

Skylor and Brynne were forced to stop their forward run, men jumping in front of them. They reached for the two ladies and then shoved them out of the back door, over the debris that lay on the floor. Despite their protests and cries to stop, the two ladies were forced forward to a vehicle. Their socked feet didn't protect them from the cold of the ground and concrete sidewalk. They watched in horror as the man who had assaulted Haley approached Skylor's car and then opened it, dumping Haley into the back seat. Skylor was forced to hand over her keys even as she fought against that.

The vehicles sped away, heading for a highly densely populated area of town. Pulling onto a paved driveway, the vehicles headed around the house and stopped near the back door. The ladies were pulled from the vehicles and then forced to the basement of the home. A hidden door was opened and the ladies were shoved inside, Haley dropped to one of the rough bunks, still unconscious. The door was slammed and locked, leaving Skylor and Brynne to stare at it, stare at one another, and then stare at Haley. Neither had any idea of what had just happened and certainly had no idea who the men were or what they wanted.

An hour later, Joe approached the house, ringing the door bell at the front door. He frowned when no one answered. He stepped to where he could see the garage and the driveway. Joe frowned as he spotted Haley's car sitting there where it always did. He walked around to the back door, pausing as he saw the damage that had been done. His hand reached to draw his weapon, stepping carefully over the debris and searching through the house. Joe paused at the kitchen table, staring at the three half-eaten bowls of stew and then searching for who might have been there. His finger touched the two jackets that lay on the couch, recognizing them as Skylor's and Brynne's. Joe drew in a deep breath. He had three ladies missing, two who had already been through enough. He drew out his phone, calling in whoever it was that he needed to.

Josh's foot hit the brake pedal in his truck in a vicious manner as he saw the emergency vehicles that lined the road outside of his home. He shoved the door open and ran towards the driveway, stopped in his tracks by an officer.

"What's going on? Where's Haley?" Josh was almost frantic with his worry about his sister.

The officer kept a hand on Josh's shoulder, looking past him as Ben ran towards them.

"She's not here, Josh. We don't know where she is. Joe appeared here to speak with her and found her missing." His voice held the compassion that he felt. This family didn't need this, he decided, and knew that all of the force would be out there looking for the three ladies. And they would find them. He just prayed that they would be alive when they did so.

"Josh? What's going on?" Ben slid to a halt similar to what Josh had done. His hand reached for his son's shoulder. "Where's Haley?" Ben had a sudden fear for his only daughter. "Josh?"

"I don't know, Dad. I just got here and found this. Is Joe here?" Josh turned to the officer, seeing his nod of confirmation. He stepped away from the police tape that shut off their access to their driveway, drawing his father with him. "Dad? Did you talk with Haley today?"

"I did, around noon. What about you?" Ben watched his son closely, seeing the fear that was prominent in his eyes.

"I did, about two hours ago. She was fine, working on something she said. I don't get it. Who did this?" Josh turned as he heard another vehicle and saw the three Koyle brothers walking towards them. "Why are they here?"

The Koyle brothers stopped beside the two men, their gaze flickering between the men and the activity around the house. Arlyn and Briar shared a deep look, fear for their wives growing. The two ladies had headed this way, they knew, wanting to spend time with Haley.

"Boys? You're here?" Ben spoke quietly before his eyes slid closed. "Skylor and Brynne? They were here?"

"We think so. They were heading this way today. Skylor said that they felt really burdened for Haley." Arlyn's heart was in a muddle, fear for his wife uppermost but also acknowledging that God had the ladies in His hands.

"They were?" Josh turned back to watch the activity, seeing Joe standing outside of the house and deep in conversation with an officer. "That means that if Haley is missing, they may well be too."

Joe stared around the area. There was no evidence of what had happened to the ladies, other than that they had disappeared. And he wanted to know exactly where they were. Joe had turned slightly to watch the road, seeing the five men waiting for word. He prayed for them. He didn't have good news for any of them and that troubled him. Joe turned back to the house, deep in thought. He wanted to know what had happened and that didn't seem to be happening at the present time. He turned back to the driveway and then walked slowly towards the men. Ducking under the police tape, Joe hesitated for a moment before he approached them.

"Joe?" Ben spoke for the group, taking the lead in that. "What happened? Where are our ladies?" Ben didn't realize that he had grouped the three ladies under his sentence in an effort to try and protect them.

Joe shook his head, a hand resting on his weapon. Someone was out there and watching them and he wanted that person. It just wouldn't happen right then, he was all too aware of that.

Chapter 12

The five men didn't move, their eyes glued to Joe's face as he hesitated. They were suddenly afraid for the ladies.

"Joe?" Cayce spoke at last, unable to keep quiet. "What aren't you telling us? If you don't speak with us, I am fully prepared to enter your crime scene even if you arrest me." Cayce was angry, angrier than he had been at any time, even with what his brothers had gone through. He just wished and prayed that he would remember why this was all happening.

"The ladies are not there, Cayce. The back door has been broken in. Ben, you'll need to find someone to repair the frame and replace the door once we're done."

Josh nodded. As a carpenter, he could and would do that.

"I'll look after it." Josh's face was hard. "What else?"

"They didn't have any outwear with them, not even boots." Joe didn't spare the men, knowing that he couldn't. He had to be honest with them. "It looks as if they were sharing a meal when it all went down." Joe hesitated before he walked away. He would have more questions for the men, including the Koyle brothers but for now, he needed to be elsewhere. Joe knew that the men would be in touch with him over the next few hours.

Cayce watched Joe leave before he turned to the others.

"We need to find them. Where would we start to even look?" Cayce was frustrated and also deeply worried. He eyed his brothers, seeing the worry and fear that was open on their faces. "Arlyn? Briar? Where would we start?"

Arlyn shrugged. His thoughts were on Skylor, wondering where she was and just praying for her safety. He knew the character of the men who were after Cayce and Haley. He and Skylor had faced them and won with God's help. Arlyn's attention turned to Cayce, seeing the worry and fear that was evident on his face. Cayce was a quiet man, he knew, the quietest of the three of them. To see his emotions on his face was not common but he could understand why.

"I don't know, Cayce. I really don't know. God knows where they are and what it will take to find them. I just pray that they are all right." Arlyn shared a look with Briar, knowing how his brother would be feeling. He felt his father's hand on his shoulder and looked around. Ben and Josh had walked away, their shoulders slumping with their worry and fear.

"Where are we meeting, Dad?" Briar barely waited for his father to respond before he was running towards Josh and Ben, causing those two men to spin in fear. "Ben? Josh? Come with us. We're meeting at Dad's to try and make some plans. I know from experience that the teams will be here for a while yet. Joe will track us down."

—

Josh nodded before he reached for his father's arm, leading him to his truck and tucking him inside. He slipped behind the wheel of his truck, his eyes on his home. All he could do at present was pray for his sister and the other ladies, leaving them in God's hands. His thoughts then turned to Cayce. Josh sighed to himself as he thought through what he knew of Cayce. He decided then that he would try and model his life after the humbleness that he saw in Cayce, determining to speak with him at some point about how he did it.

Bessie turned into her husband's hug, a troubled look on her face. She could tell from his look at her that the news was not good and that caused fear and trouble to rise in her heart.

"Ardan? Where are the girls?" Bessie saw Anna approaching the four younger men, hugs delivered to all of them including Josh. Anna held onto the triplets just a little bit longer than she usually would.

"We have no idea. Joe isn't saying much as yet. He'll head this way once he can." Ardan hugged his wife, his eyes on Ben. "Ben? We'll find them. That is a guarantee."

Ben nodded soberly, not sure what to say. He was more than a little worried about his daughter and of course the other two ladies. He appreciated what Ardan was saying but that didn't solve the mystery of where the ladies were or who had them or if they were safe. Ben's fear was that the ladies were hurt and would not return home.

"I know that we will, Ardan. I just don't want to wait." Ben drew in a deep, shuddering breath. "I'm afraid for them, Ardan, Bessie. How do we find them?" Ben was repeating himself in some ways, well aware that the couple with him felt the same. He turned as he felt a hand on his shoulder.

Joe stood by the older adults, concern on his face. There had been little evidence to find in Ben's home. What concerned him was the spots of blood that they found on the floor. One of the ladies had been injured. The officers and crime scene team had discussed it among themselves. The consensus was that it was likely Haley. The other ladies were collateral to her kidnapping. All they could do was pray for them and then struggle to find them.

Cayce turned as he heard Joe's voice before he walked out of the house and away from it. He didn't want to hear that Joe had no idea where the ladies were. That much was obvious to anyone who had half a brain, he decided. Cayce felt a presence beside him and looked around. There was no one there but he was sure that he had heard footsteps walking in step with him. He looked up. All Cayce could do at that time thank God for His protection. Cayce would not go to anyone for help. That was not his character to do that. He was always ready to reach out to others and provide help and care when it was needed. Cayce just didn't ask for help. He wanted to stay anonymous and in the background. Only this time, God had called him out of his comfort zone and into the forefront of whatever battle that they were involved in.

—

Briar and Arlyn watched their brother walk away, their aunt's arms linked with theirs. They wanted to go after him but sensed that he needed to be on his own. That hurt but they could understand that. They had felt the same way.

Joe watched as Cayce walked away from his parents' home before he was running after him. A hand on Cayce's arm halted his forward progress. Cayce spun, his eyes huge with fear before he jerked his arm away from Joe.

"Cayce? Where are you heading?" Joe didn't confront Cayce directly. He knew better than to do that.

"Where am I heading? I have no idea. Home, I guess." Cayce's words were clipped and short, the anger that he was feeling evident in his voice. "Or else to wherever it is that the ladies are. Do you know where that is?" Cayce was challenging Joe and they both knew it.

"I don't know that, Cayce. We have no idea who took them. The security feed was damaged earlier today and no one was aware of it." Joe rubbed at his cheek. "Can we find somewhere to talk? I need to go back over everything with you."

"And we can go over it ad infinitum and still not be clear as to what happened." Cayce stared down the street. "Joe? That car? It's coming too fast."

Joe spun and then threw himself at Cayce, sending both of them to the lawn of the house that they had stopped in front of and then rolling them away from the sidewalk. They could feel the rush of air and the squeal of tires as the car mounted the sidewalk and just missed them, disappearing into the distance.

Joe sat up, a hand keeping Cayce down on the ground. He drew in a shaky breath. That had been much too close. Cayce shoved away from Joe and sprung to his feet, running to the road and staring at the spot where the car had disappeared. Someone had just tried to kill either himself or Joe. And he wanted that person.

Chapter 13

Joe's hand once more stopped Cayce in his tracks. His phone was out as he called in the incident, frustration and anger evident on his face. He didn't want any harm or any more harm to come to. Cayce than had already happened.

"Cayce? You are not chasing down that car. You don't have a vehicle for one thing. And for another thing, it's already disappeared." Joe looked around, not sure what had just happened other than someone had just tried to kill one of them. His thoughts were that it was Cayce.

"Who was that, Joe? Do you even know?" Cayce's anger bubbled over in his words. He spun to stare at Joe, seeing the compassion mixed with anger on Joe's face.

"No, I don't. It happened to quickly, Cayce. Now, we need to get you back to your parents' home where I pray that you will be safe." Joe shoved Cayce forward, finding that man reluctant to leave where they were. "Move, Cayce. Go back to your parents." He waved at a patrol officer, pointing to where they had landed on the grass. He kept pushing Cayce forward at a rapid pace, watching as the door to the house opened and then close after Cayce before he strode back towards the crime scene.

The occupants of the house stared at Cayce, seeing the anger on his face and the mud that covered some of his clothing. He shoved past them and headed up the stairs to his old bedroom. He knew that there were clothes there that he could change into. Cayce just didn't want to. He turned as he heard a tap at the door and then his brothers entered.

"Cayce? What just happened?" Arlyn stared at his brother, not sure what had happened but he knew something had.

"Someone just tried to run Joe and I down. He shoved me out of the way." Cayce ran his hands down his face. "The car just missed us and then just disappeared into the horizon." Cayce shuddered at the close call. "Who is after me? Or are they after Haley? Or one of our parents?"

Arlyn stopped pacing at Cayce's words. That wasn't something that he had even considered. He turned to find Briar nodding.

"Briar? You've thought about this?" Arlyn's voice was low. He really didn't believe that could be a possibility.

Briar nodded. Brynne had come up with the idea and had repeatedly stated it. He had come to believe that it was a definite possibility.

"Brynne's convinced that this is a possibility. I must say, I have to agree with her." Briar studied his younger brother. "Cayce? What are your thoughts?"

Cayce shrugged. He had no idea if this was true or not but it was a definite possibility.

"It's possible you know. We need to talk with Mom and Dad and Ben to see what their thoughts are." He sank down onto his childhood bed, his head buried in his heads. "I wish that I could remember everything."

"God will cause you to remember when the time is right. You can't remember anything?" Arlyn sat beside him, shoulders touching, wanting to comfort his brother but not sure how to do that.

"Not really. I have fleeting images but nothing concrete. The images just are not clear enough." Cayce drew in a deep breath. "How do we do this? How do we find our ladies?"

Arlyn and Briar shared a glance, not surprised at how Cayce had claimed Haley. They were a couple, everyone could see that. They just didn't know if that couple would ever happen.

"Let's find the others and see what they have to say." Briar hauled his brother to his feet and then shoved him towards the door and down the stairs.

The three younger men found the four older adults in the kitchen, mingling around the table. The brothers stopped for a moment, searching the faces of their loved ones. The older adults turned to face the brothers, not knowing what had happened and why Cayce had appeared back so quickly.

"Cayce? What happened, son?" Ardan finally spoke for the group.

"Someone tried to run Joe and me down. I don't know who or why." Cayce's anger had abated to some degree. He fully realized that he had to release his anger but he didn't want to. He could feel God's prompts in his heart to do that.

"What?" Bessie came to hug her son. "And he's working it?"

"He is. I wish this was all over and we knew who and why and that the ladies were back with us." Cayce looked up, blinking rapidly before he turned once more and walked away. Arlyn and Briar flanked him, Arlyn pointing towards his truck. "Where are we heading?"

"We'll drive around for a while, Cayce. They may appear just like you two did." Arlyn didn't expect that to happen but he could still pray that it would. He was planning on staying at Cayce's that night and he didn't need to ask Briar to know that he would be doing the same.

"That would be nice." Cayce stared out of the side window of the truck. "We need to call in help, guys. Joe's not getting anywhere."

"I spoke with Samuel earlier today. He said that he would have Blackie and Simon start working on what we had. And Emma called. I gave her all the information that we have." Briar was sober as he spoke. These were friends who were either investigators or in the case of Emma, finding people who no one else could.

"That's good. When are they planning on coming to town?" Cayce gave a grim smile as his brothers laughed. They didn't have to say much. They could almost read one another's minds.

"Tomorrow or the next day. They want to meet with us. They are praying for our ladies." Briar passed on the words that Samuel had spoken to him. "They are very concerned about them."

—

"They would be. They went through enough, particularly Emma and Abe." Arlyn walked away, heading for the outside, shrugging into his jacket as he did so. He missed Skylor greatly and wanted her back. He had to yield to God, though, having complete confidence that God would protect their ladies and bring them home.

The next morning, Samuel, Blackie and Simon walked towards Ardan's home, knowing that was where they were all meeting. Ardan had reached out to him the night before, just to bring him up to the moment on what they knew. They knew that Abe and Emma were already inside the house. They shared a look, knowing that this would be a difficult conversation with the family, particularly with Cayce.

Abe passed them as he headed towards his truck, pausing for a moment. He was not surprised to see the three men. They had all been there for Arlyn and Briar. It was only common sense that they would be there for Cayce.

"Fellows?" Abe paused, his eyes searching the area around them. Someone was out there and he knew that it was only a matter of time before they moved in on Cayce.

"Off on a search, Abe?" Blackie gave a grin before he sobered. "Emma's inside?"

"She is. They're waiting for you three. I'm off on a search myself." Abe waved as he walked away, heading for the black SUV that sat waiting for him. He slipped into the front passenger seat, sober as he studied to area around the house once more.

Murphy, his business partner, stared at Abe and then at the house. His fingers tapped on the steering wheel. He knew that Ian and Nathaniel were in the back seat of their SUV and that Joseph, Luke, Matt, and Micah were in the SUV parked right behind them.

"How are they?" Murphy's quiet voice broke through the silence in the vehicle.

"They're hurting. They didn't expect this to happen, not to their third son. Arlyn and Briar are grieving and angry. That's to be expected. We know to a certain extent how they feel." Abe turned to face the other three. "Emma's confirmed that address for us. Let's head that way and see what we can discover. I spoke with Joe earlier. He's heading that way as well, just to provide support for us." Abe really didn't expect to find the ladies but he was praying that they would.

"We do know somewhat of that." Ian spoke for the men. "They have the support that they need, just as we did, but it doesn't help when your lady is missing."

Murphy pulled his vehicle to a stop where he could watch the house in question. There was no movement around it and that didn't surprise them. He shared a look with Abe, who was out of the vehicle and approaching Luke who nodded towards the house. Abe looked around as he sensed a new person nearby and nodded at Joe.

"This is the house, Abe?" Joe didn't doubt that it was. It just surprised him.

"It is. Emma has confirmed that it is. Don't ask how she did that. You know better than to ask that." Abe gave a quick smile. Emma could find people, addresses, and information that no one else could. She just couldn't explain it other than it was God.

Joe studied the house. He sighed to himself. He was not expecting this house or these people. Joe knew the people who lived there. He didn't think that they were involved in crime, but then again, they could well be hiding behind a facade.

The three men spun as they heard running footsteps and Luke appeared, beckoning them to come with him. They ran after him, frowns on their faces. Sliding to a halt, Abe stared at his team and then the three ladies they were surrounding.

"Guys? What's going on? Where did you find the ladies?" Abe studied the ladies, seeing the fear on Skylor's and Brynne's faces. He was unable to read Haley. There was a huge bruise on her face and she swayed on her feet, kept upright by Matt's arm around her. He knew that Matt was assessing her as he held her upright, being the paramedic on his team.

"They were just walking down the street. I haven't asked them anything yet." Nathaniel spoke up. "Joe, that's what you need to do. But for now? We need to get them to medical aid, particularly Haley."

Abe nodded before he spoke with Joe.

"Joe, we'll head for the hospital. Will you contact the families?" Abe was away before Joe could do nothing more than nod.

Joe sighed before he reached for his phone. He would need the search warrants for that house and that meant calling in officers and a crime scene team. He

---

was frustrated at having a third brother involved in a mystery that only seemed to be deepening without any end or solution in sight. Joe looked up, begging God for answers that didn't seem to be coming. He had to admit that God was in control once more and the answer would come in His timing.

Tucked into the vehicles, Skylor and Brynne looked around. They were safe, they were well aware of that, and had confidence that Abe and his team would keep them safe.

"Joseph? Our guys?" Skylor's voice was hesitant and barely audible.

"They're at their parents. They're fine other than being very worried about you two." Joseph eyed them. "How did you get away?"

"We just walked away. It was so bizarre." Skylor drew in a deep breath. "We had been locked into a cell. Today, the door was unlocked. Haley insisted that we leave. She almost ran for the room as best as she could. It was so bizarre. There were three jackets hanging on hooks near the back door and also shoes that were our size."

"It was so strange. Everything fit us. It is as if someone knew what size we wore and made sure that they were available." Brynne also drew in a shaking breath. "God does this, doesn't He? He provides angels or people who can help us even when we don't know they are there."

Murphy pulled the SUV to a halt near the Emergency entrance to the hospital. He shifted on his

---

seat, eyes studying the area around them. He was uneasy and that meant danger was near to them.

Joseph and the other two men rushed the ladies into the hospital, startling the charge nurse. At his words, she pointed to a room and he rushed the two ladies into there before he and Luke stood outside of the room, protecting them.

Abe turned as he heard the hurried footsteps and nodded. Haley was already in a room with a physician heading that way. He was frustrated. Abe had watched a vehicle follow them before it sped away from the hospital. That the ladies had escaped had been noted. That worried him.

Joe tucked his phone away as he walked towards the house. An officer had run towards him, waving the necessary search warrants. The man who had been watching the house for the owner paced towards him. He had not been there for a month or so, he stated, having been sick in the hospital. The owners had been okay with that, he stated. What had happened was his next question. He had work to do here even though he really needed to be at the hospital to take the ladies' statements. That had had to be delegated to another investigator.

Chapter 15

Ben and Josh moved rapidly towards the room where Haley was being examined. All they knew was that she was safe and under care. They hesitated in the doorway before the nurse turned and beckoned them forward. Neither one moved for a moment before Ben's hand landed on Josh's shoulder and gently shoved his son forward. The two men stood where they were out of the way of the medical staff who were working rapidly around Haley.

Josh's eyes landed on his sister's face. Anger grew inside of him. He had not been aware that she had been assaulted. The bruise covered a good portion of one side of her face. Josh winced, knowing how it must hurt.

Ben's arm rested across his son's shoulders. He prayed for his daughter and then his son. He drew in a deep breath, ready to ask his questions. The physician looked around and then pointed towards a corner of the room.

"Doc?" Ben's voice was quiet even though it was filled with worry and fear.

"Ben? Josh? What happened to her?" The physician, James Austen, turned to study Haley.

"She disappeared last night with Skylor and Brynne. We don't know what all happened to them. What about her face?" Josh spoke for the two of them.

—

"Haley will be going for imaging soon. I can't tell if her jaw is broken or not. It's that swollen. She should have been treated after it happened."

"It should of but it wasn't. Now we have to deal with it." Ben walked away to the stretcher, a hand coming out to rest on his daughter's hair as he prayed for her.

Haley shifted restlessly as she felt someone touch her. She thought that she should recognize the touch but pain was driving her down into a dark well that she didn't expect to ever come back from.

Josh took a look at his sister and then turned away. He had sworn all his life to protect her and this time? He hadn't been able to. He watched as she was moved away to the imaging department. Josh headed to find Cayce. Cayce needed to be with Haley and Haley needed him to be with her. They were a couple, whether they had acknowledged it or not.

Ben stood for a moment in the waiting room, his eyes searching for someone who he could blame. He shook his head before he turned to find Josh and Cayce standing beside him.

"Cayce?" Ben's voice held a brokenness that was not usually in it.

"Ben? How is Haley?" Cayce was worried about her. He had had an opportunity to speak with Joe but that man had not said much. Joe needed to speak with the ladies before he could say much.

"She's hurting, Cayce. James isn't sure if her jaw is broken or not." Ben eyed Cayce as he saw the look of pain cross his face. "We'll get you back to her, son. You need each other."

Cayce nodded before he turned to walk from the waiting room, his hands clenched into fists. If the man who had assaulted Haley had been standing in front of him, he might well have retaliated. And that was not Cayce. He was a peaceful man, working in the background to keep the peace and make everyone feel safe.

Arlyn and Briar followed their brother, pacing in tandem with him. They were all hurting. The two older brothers had not yet been able to see their brides but knew that would happen soon, once Joe had taken their statements. They were afraid of what they would hear.

"Cayce? Let us pray with you." Briar finally reached out a hand and stopped his brother. "You need to hear our prayers."

Cayce paused, his head dropping forward. He rubbed at his eyes, willing the tears to disappear.

"Haley's hurting, Briar. She may have a broken jaw." Cayce looked up at his brothers to see anger fleeting across their faces. "Ben said that she's in imaging right now for an x-ray."

Arlyn nodded. He had wondered about that, praying for both his brother and Haley. He knew that God was in control. They had to trust Him, no matter what they faced. He and Skylor had had to learn that over and over during what they had gone through.

—

"You're going in to see her." Josh had appeared. "Come on, Cayce. She's back in her room." Josh's hand on Cayce's shoulder directed him towards the rooms. He paused at the door, his eyes on Cayce. That man was connected with his sister in a way that no one else was. They were far from through with what they were facing.

"It's not right, Arlyn. I shouldn't be here." Cayce tried to move away but found that Ben was standing behind him. "Ben?"

"You're part of our lives, Cayce. Haley has a different tone in her voice when she talks about you. That tells me that you are important to her." Ben's hand went up as Cayce's mouth opened to protest. "It's true, Cayce. Now, in with the two of you." Ben reached past his son to shove at the door. He walked in and towards his daughter, leaving the two men to stare at one another before they came in as well.

Haley moved restlessly, hearing footsteps and fearing the worst. She thought that it was her father's voice that she heard speaking with her but how could that be, unless he had been taken as well. Haley felt the movement of the stretcher as she was moved to a medical bed on the medical floor.

Ben finally left the hospital, knowing that he had to. He pulled Josh with him. It was late at night and they had been granted the time to spend with Haley. Cayce just refused to leave, simply stating that he needed to be there. He had not turned as the two men walked away, not seeing the police officer standing outside of Haley's room, on guard for now until Joe could speak with her.

Cayce pulled a chair up closer to the bed, begging his Heavenly Father for healing and protection for his lady. He wasn't able to understand why this had happened. He had felt eyes watching them when they had been outside and also when they had been moving around the hospital. Cayce was well aware that the person or persons didn't mean this good, only harm, and only God could intervene.

Haley's eyes flickered open as she felt a hand on hers, the grip familiar and strong. She shifted her head slightly, pain shooting through it, as she struggled to see.

"Haley?" Cayce kept his voice low. "Haley? Sweetheart? Are you waking up?"

Haley squinted at him. Of course, Cayce would be here.

"Where am I?" Haley's voice was barely audible, pain keeping her from speaking in her normal tone.

"You're in the hospital. You and Skylor and Brynne escaped today. The day that you were missing was the longest of my life." His hand tightened on hers.

"It was? I don't remember. Don't leave me, Cayce. I need you in my life." Haley slept, not realizing that she had bared her heart to him.

Cayce's smile was tender yet bitter at the same time. He didn't understand what they were going through and was not even sure that they ever would. His eyes closed as he prayed and then slept, not hearing

—

the soft footsteps of the nurses as they entered, monitored Haley's vitals, and then moved away once more.

Chapter 16

Early the next morning, Joe shoved open the hospital room door and paused. He shook his head. He should have known that Cayce would be there. Joe stood at the end of the bed, watching Haley as she stared back at him.

"Joe? What happened? I don't remember anything." Haley could barely get the words out of her mouth. Her free hand played with the IV line that ran to the back of her hand.

"You don't? That's not what I wanted to hear." Joe sighed, knowing that she was speaking the truth. "You don't remember anything at all?"

Haley barely shook her head, not able to do much more than that.

"Is my jaw broken, Joe? I haven't been told and I need to know." Haley blinked back tears, frustrated, scared, and worried all in one.

"No, it's just badly bruised. It will hurt as if it is broken." Joe's gaze shifted to Cayce who had awakened and was watching Haley, not saying anything. Cayce's heart and love for the lady were on his face for all to see. Joe was not surprised at that. "Cayce?"

Haley's eyes shifted to watch Cayce, surprised to see him there.

"Cayce?" Her voice was slightly more audible, a question obvious in it.

"Haley? You're awake at last." He ignored Joe, reaching to drop a kiss on her forehead. "I'm so glad that you're back." Cayce struggled with his emotions before he walked from the room. He needed some space from the lady whom he loved deeply. He paused outside of the door, to turn his head to stare at said door before he walked away. Pacing the hallway on the medical floor, Cayce was lost in thought, trying to think through what had happened.

His phone in his hand, Cayce paused to study the text messages that had come through. The first one had been blank. The second one showed an explosion. The third one was a direct threat against him, simply stating that he was next. Cayce had forwarded the text messages on to Joe but had not had a chance to speak with him. He heard footsteps behind him and moved towards the closed door to his right.

The man approaching Cayce kept his head down and his ball cap pulled down over his face as much as he could. The hood on his jacket was also over his head, effectively blocking any image of his face. His feet were set down carefully as he crept closer to Cayce, finding that man not watching around him at all.

Cayce tucked away his phone, praying for his lady and then for himself. He wanted this over. He wanted to explore his feelings for Haley and hers for him. He fingered the ring that he had in his pocket, wanting to place it on her finger but not sure if she would even accept it. Cayce didn't hear the footsteps that picked up their pace as the man neared Cayce.

A sudden violent shove against the closed door sent Cayce flying into the darkened room, barely able to keep to his feet. He spun to face the man, his hands raising into the air as he saw the vicious knife that the man held in front on him. Cayce backed away until he could not back away any further, the bed hitting him from behind.

The man stared at Cayce, an angry, contemptuous look on his face. He stepped closer, his feet set down carefully on the tiled floor. Unable to move away from the man, Cayce jerked backwards as the knife swiped towards his abdomen. Shock and pain shone on his face as the knife found its target in his abdomen and then the man stepped backwards, wiping the knife blade on a towel that he grabbed from the bedside table.

Cayce's hand found the wound as his knees buckled and he slumped to the floor. He didn't seen the man turn and leave or see the shadow that moved towards him and bent over him to lay a hand on Cayce's head. Cayce was sprawled on his back, unconscious. His head had hit hard as he landed on the tiled floor and with that block and the pain, he just slipped away into darkness.

An hour later, Joe went looking for Cayce. He and Haley had spoken at length as to what was happening to her and Cayce before she had finally slept. Joe had spent time updating the file and then working through his emails. Stretching as he rose, he stepped from the room and frowned. Cayce had been gone for too long, he decided, and began a search.

Josh and Briar approached Joe, frowning at him.

"Joe? You're on a search?" Josh spoke for the duo.

"I am. Cayce walked away from Haley's room an hour ago and hasn't returned. And he's not answering my call or text." Joe was becoming increasingly concerned. His phone was out again as he strode through the hallway, trying to connect with Cayce.

A sound of a phone ringing stopped the three men in their tracks. They shared a look before Joe hit the closed door in an almost violent manner and then searched for the light switch with his right hand. The light almost blinded them for a moment before Briar gave a cry and sprang forward, to drop to his knees beside his brother. A shaking hand reached for Cayce's wrist, relief washing through him as he felt his brother's pulse, as weak as it was.

Josh ran for the nurse's station, his calls startling the nurses and bringing a physician from a room. The physician was doing his morning rounds and once he heard Josh's jumbled words, he ran towards the room and dropped to his knees as well beside Cayce.

Josh stood back, an arm around Briar's shoulders as they watched the hurried activity around Cayce. Joe had strode from the room, heading for the security officer who stood nearby. A nod from that man and they were running for the security office to find the video feed on that particular area of the hospital.

Cayce was shifted to a stretcher and the stretcher was pushed rapidly for the surgical suites. He needed urgent surgery, that much was obvious. The physician, the on-call surgeon in fact, moved with quick steps ahead of the stretcher, calling for imaging in the suite and then for an operating room to be prepared.

Briar stared after his brother, a hand covering his mouth. He had troubling controlling his emotions, knowing that he had to call his family, but not wanting to make that call. Briar didn't realize that Arlyn, Skylor, and Brynne had appeared, standing back and watching the activity before Brynne moved in to hug him.

"Briar? What happened? Who was that?" Brynne's hug and soft words roused Briar from his shock.

Briar hugged his wife back, his eyes still on the elevator doors that had closed behind his brother.

"Cayce. He was stabbed. I don't know who or when." He felt Arlyn's arms across his shoulders and Skylor's soft prayer. "We need to call Mom and Dad."

"It's been done, Briar." Arlyn spoke, his head turning for a moment. "Where's Haley?"

"She's still asleep, I think." Briar was torn. He needed to follow his brother but he also needed to find his brother's lady.

Skylor and Brynne shared a look, hugged their guys, and then walked away with Josh to find Haley was still sound asleep. It was good, they declared. If she hadn't been, she would have been on her feet and running after Cayce. It was obvious to everyone that those two shared a bond.

—

Chapter 17

Haley roused as she heard conversation in her room. She frowned at the anxiety and fear that she heard in the words. Her eyes opened to find Josh standing beside her bed, a hand on her arm.

"Josh?" Haley's voice was slightly stronger than it had been. "What is going on? Where's Cayce?" When Josh didn't answer, Haley turned to the others in the room, a question on her face.

"Cayce has been hurt, Haley. He's in surgery." Skylor's hand on Haley's shoulder kept her still. "He was stabbed in an empty room down the hall from here. Joe, Josh, and Briar found him."

Haley stared at them and then reached to pull the IV line from her hand. Her dark look at Josh had him grinning before he stepped from the room. Haley was out of the bed, reaching for the bag of clothes that Brynne had held out for her and was away to dress. She winced for a moment as the act of dressing jarred her face. Tears briefly tracked down her face before she angrily swiped them away. All she could do at the present time was beg God for Cayce's life and healing. She had grown to love that man and knew from his words and actions that he loved her deeply even in such a short period of time.

Skylor and Brynne linked arms with Haley as they moved from the room and towards the elevator. Ben had appeared, drawn there by his son's phone call. He studied his daughter and her friends and then studied his son. To say that Josh was deeply worried and afraid went without saying. Ben watched his daughter carefully, seeing that she was indeed in pain but not as much as she had been. The two men in Haley's life followed the three ladies, heading for where they would find the Koyle family.

Bessie was on her feet, reaching to hug Haley and then draw her down beside her. Anna's arm went around Haley as well. The two other ladies found their men, wrapped in the men's arms. Ardan approached Ben and Josh, pointing to seats in a corner.

"What do you know, Ardan?" Ben broke the silence between the trio.

"Not a lot. Cayce was shoved into a darkened room about an hour before he was found. If Joe had not gone looking for him, we don't know how long that he would have been there. The surgeon was on the floor and that is a God moment if there ever was one. He was able to assess Cayce and bring him right up for treatment." Ardan was angry. He felt justified in his anger but also knew that his anger was fuelled by fear for his son. No one could explain why it had taken that long for Cayce to be found. Ardan was thankful that he had been found before something more dire had happened but it didn't help.

"An hour?" Ben sat back, shock on his face. "How bad?"

"The surgeon was noncommittal until he was able to assess Cayce in the operating room. It's been about an hour or so since he spoke with us. Joe was around but had to leave." Ardan was sober, afraid that he would lose his youngest son but also aware that God was in control.

Josh's head bowed as he prayed for his friend and the man whom he suspected would be his brother-in-law. He felt a hand on his arm and looked sideways. Haley had moved to sit beside him, her arm wrapping around his. Her head rested against his shoulder, drawing strength from her beloved brother.

"Okay, sis?" Josh tilted his head to look at her.

Haley shrugged. She had no idea how she was to feel. Her emotions were in a turmoil, she had to admit. All she wanted was to see Cayce standing in front of her, well and uninjured. That wasn't about to happen. Haley looked up as she saw someone stop in front of her. Joe stood there, a shuttered look on his face.

"Joe? What do you know?" Haley's voice was growing stronger even though it hurt to speak.

"Not a lot, Haley. I'm sorry. The man kept his face hidden." Joe was frustrated at the turn of events. This was not helping to solve anything. He had reached out to friends for help but so far, nothing had come back to him.

"That's okay, Joe. It's not your fault." Haley's eyes closed as she slept, her strength depleted.

Josh shifted so that he could wrap an arm around his sister, cradling her against him. His eyes closed as he thought through the years, knowing that their relationship was changing, as well it should.

—

Joe slid down onto a chair, his eyes on his note pad as he read through the notes from his various investigations. He felt as if he was getting nowhere with any of his cases. The incessant vibrating of his phone had him reaching for it and then he was running for the stairs. Word had come in that had something to do with Cayce and Haley, and Joe needed to meet with that person.

Josh, Briar, and Arlyn watched Joe run from the room before they shared looks and simply shrugged. Josh's arm tightened around his sister, trying desperately to convey to her that he was watching out for her and would protect her with his life if that became necessary.

Haley shifted in how she was sitting, her eyes opening as pain hit her. She looked up to see a nurse in front of her, handing over a small paper cup with her pain medications and also handing her a foam cup of water with a lit and straw. Haley thanked her softly before she looked around at all the people who were there. She frowned at the couple who were approaching them, not recognizing them.

Briar looked around and then he and Arlyn were on their feet, heading for the couple. The lady hugged them before she moved past them to hug their brides. She then turned to Haley, finding a questioning look on Haley's face.

"Haley? My name is Emma Finlay. I am friends with the Koyles as is my husband. Let me explain. My husband, Abe, has a security team. They do training now instead of protecting people. They were involved with both Arlyn and Briar's adventures as we term them. As for me? I have a business where I find information and people. And before you ask, I can't explain how I do it other than God." Emma perched on the edge of a chair seat. "You're waiting for word on Cayce. We'll speak with him when we can. But for now? May I pray with you? You need all that we can give you. That is what we are offering, Haley. We want to help you. And we never ask for any money from our friends. We consider you our friend." Emma grinned at her for a moment. "I can see that I have taken you aback. That's unfortunately the effect I have on people."

Haley gave a half-smile, not sure if she should believe this lady or not. She looked up to see Skylor and Brynne nodding, wide smiles on their faces. She sighed. Emma must be a good friend for these two ladies to look like that.

Chapter 18

The surgeon pulled off his surgical cap and then pulled his mask down below his chin. Cayce was now in recovery, the wound stitched back together. They had worked to stop the bleeding after some time and searching. He was praising God that nothing vital had been touched. The feeling was that Cayce was moving backwards away from the knife.

He paused at Cayce's side, a thoughtful look on his face. He turned at last, knowing that Cayce would soon be in a bed in a room and then his family could be with him. He shook his head as he headed for the waiting room, knowing that his family could be with him.

Ardan looked up as he heard footsteps and rose to greet the surgeon. He heard his family rising and standing in a semi-circle around him. Sounds from others in the waiting room just faded as Ardan concentrated on what the surgeon would have to say.

"Doc? How is Cayce?" Bessie wrapped an arm around her husband and then around Anna. She could see Ben and Josh with their arms around Haley as she stood, wavering on her feet but determined to hear what the physician had to say.

"Cayce is very lucky or should we say, God had His hand on him. Cayce seemed to have been moving away from the knife. There were no vital organs nicked or sliced. There was a lot of bleeding but we were able to stop it. He'll need time to heal. For now, he is in Recovery and will before about another hour or so. The nurse will come and find you when he's in a room." The surgeon paused for a moment before he looked up and then walked away.

The Koyle family looked at one another before the men moved away, leaving the ladies to wait for what, they weren't sure. Haley stared at the men and then at the ladies, wanting to join them but not sure if she should. She felt Emma's hand on her arm drawing her towards the other ladies. The ladies all looked at one another before their heads all bowed and they began to pray for Cayce and his healing. Then, they began to pray for Haley. Haley was surprised at that, not expecting it at all but accepting it.

Skylor paced away from the ladies, Emma at her side, to head for the cafeteria and find something for the ladies to eat. Emma stopped for a moment to take a call, a frown appearing on her face before she tucked away her phone. At some point, she would need to find Abe and see what his thoughts were, although she had a good idea what they were.

Two hours later, Ardan and Bessie stood at Cayce's bedside. Both of them had hands resting on their son's arms but he was not rousing. They had been warned to expect that, given the general anesthesia. Joe had appeared just after he had been moved to the room, frustrated that he could not speak with Cayce yet. He needed to do that and soon, preferably before he spoke with anyone.

Late that night, Haley crept into Cayce's room. She had been in to see him before but this time, she was on her own. She had sent her family home and knew that Cayce's family had left as well after praying

---

for both of them. Her hand reached for Cayce's, surprised to find that his had tightened on hers.

Cayce was rousing, even though it was taking longer than it should have. He clung to the hand that had reached out for him. It wasn't one of the ladies in his family. His eyes opened as he searched for the lady he loved. Cayce was surprised to see her standing beside him and holding his hand, her eyes closed. He frowned at the bruising on her face before he remembered. He just couldn't remember what he had gone and done that landed him in a hospital bed.

"Haley? Sweetheart?" Cayce had to clear his throat to get his words out.

Haley's eyes sprang open, startled at him speaking. She was not expecting that.

"Cayce? You're awake. How are you feeling? And who did this to you?" Haley reached to give him a hug.

Cayce hugged her back, before he reached for her hand.

"Don't leave me, Haley. Marry me." Cayce knew that this was not the place for a proposal but he was that desperate to know that she would accept him.

"Cayce? Are you sure?" Haley was desperate as well.

"I am, Haley. I love you. It may seem that it's too soon but it's not. Please? Marry me?" Cayce's hand opened to reveal a beautiful blue diamond ring. He sighed. "This is not how I wanted to do this."

"No, it wouldn't be." Haley bit at her bottom lip, studying the man in front on her. "I love you too, Cayce." She watched as he slid the ring onto her finger and then with one hand behind her neck pulled her down into a kiss.

"We'll figure it out, sweetheart. We'll get it figured out." Cayce grimaced with pain as he released Haley.

Haley stood with her hand over her mouth, horrified at how he was hurting. She turned and almost ran from the room, devastated that she had caused the pain, not stopping as Cayce called after her.

Cayce struggled to move from the bed, unable to do so for the pain. His head dropped back on the pillow, his eyes closing as he fought against and through the pain. His head spun for a moment before he dropped back into a well of darkness. Cayce didn't hear his father approaching his bedside.

Ardan rested a hand on his son's shoulder and prayed for him. He had spied Haley disappearing into the elevator, Josh raising a hand to him before the doors closed behind them. He was more than a little worried about Cayce and what he was facing. Something had changed with Cayce, Ardan seemed to sense and that involved Haley. He would need to wait, he knew, to find out what had happened.

Joe hesitated outside of Cayce's room, his eyes on the waiting room. It was empty, which was strange. There should be people there. He turned to the officer with him and sent him on a search.

Stepping inside the room, Joe's hand held the door open for a moment. Cayce seemed to be asleep but Joe sensed something off in the room. Danger was present. A hand reached for his weapon as he heard a soft whisper of sound. He didn't have an opportunity to more than start to turn when something heavy landed on the back of the head. Joe sprawled on the floor, unconscious. He didn't feel himself dragged into a dark corner and his handcuffs yanked from his belt and then his arms locked into them behind his back.

The eerie silence on the floor met Haley as she stepped from the elevator. She froze and then backed into the elevator, her hand hitting the button to close the door and then another button to send her back to the main floor. She ran from the elevator, desperately searching for someone, finding a security officer standing near the main door. He spun as she slid to a stop beside him, his eyes lifting towards the elevator before he ran that way, keying his mike for help.

Haley stood and watched the activity that ensued. She jumped as she felt an arm come around her and leaned into her brother's hug. Both siblings had no idea what was happening, but something had. Haley would not have reacted as she had if everything had been as it should have been.

Chapter 19

Patrol officers flooded the hospital, working with the security staff at the hospital to determine what was going on. Surprised to find the patients in their rooms, the officers stared at one another and then questioned the patients. The similar stories of a security officer ordering them to remain in their rooms puzzled the officers and also the security staff. There had been no alert that should have caused this.

Standing outside of Cayce's room, two officers hesitated. There was concern about entering but they had to go in. Reaching for the light switch, the first officer searched the room, just seeing Cayce at first. He turned as he heard a sharp cry from his companion and then holstered his weapon and dropped to his knees beside Ardan. Ardan was not responding to the shakes or questions. The officer looked up, shocked to see Joe handcuffed and nearby by, also not responding. He was on his feet, heading for the nurse's station, finding the nurses once more on duty. When questioned, the charge nurse simply stated that they were all shoved into a room and locked into it. They could not escape from it.

Transported to the Emergency department, Joe and Ardan were slow to rouse. Ardan roused first, disoriented and not sure where he was or what had happened. He shook his head when questioned.

"I don't know what happened. All I can remember is being in Cayce's room and now here."

Ardan sat up abruptly, despite the pain that coursed through his head. "Cayce? Where is he?"

"He is in room." The physician rested a hand against Ardan's shoulder. "We'll get you up there shortly. I understand that an officer was injured as well. Cayce is being moved to another room as his room is now a crime scene."

Ardan laid back on his pillow, a hand resting against his temple. Hearing commotion at the door, his hand reached out for Bessie who almost ran to him.

"Ardan? What happened? I received a call that you were hurt and to come right away."

"I was knocked out and woke up here. Cayce is fine from what I've been told." He looked past Bessie to see Haley hovering near the door. "Haley? Come in, girl. You need to be with us."

Haley shrugged as she walked cautiously into the room. She looked everywhere but at them. Bessie reached to hug the younger lady, drawing her close to her side.

"Haley? What happened?" Ardan watched her closely, sending that something had.

"I was the one." Haley sniffed, her emotions almost too much for her.

"The one? The one who did what? You didn't slug me, did you?" Ardan smiled at her, trying to relieve her emotions.

"I was the one who discovered no one on the floor. I stepped off the elevator and felt such a sense of danger and fear. I just backed into the elevator and found a security officer. I've been waiting for word that I can see Cayce. Is he okay?"

"As far as we know, he is. He's being moved to another room." Ardan looked past the two ladies to frown as Joe appeared in the doorway, staggering slightly. "Joe?"

"Ardan? How are you?" Joe paused for a moment, his eyes closing against his headache. He had been shocked, to say the least, to find that he had been knocked out and then left handcuffed.

"About the same as you. Are you sure that you should be up?" Ardan was working to control the pain but failing miserably.

"No, I don't think that I should be. Haley? Are you ready to find Cayce?" Joe reached for her hand and drew her with him. "I'm off duty but I need to find Cayce and see what he has to say. I hear that you were the one who raised the alarm."

"I guess I did. I just couldn't step any further into the waiting room. I had to leave." Haley shuddered at her remembered fear. She looked up at Joe, feeling his hand tighten on her arm. "Did I do something wrong?"

"No, you did everything right. You removed yourself from a dangerous situation. God stopped you from moving forward into something that may well have killed you." Joe punched the button in the elevator angrily. His head was pounding and he had difficulty thinking. He had been ordered to go home but had refused. His friends needed him.

———

"I guess." Haley stepped out onto the surgical floor, stunned at the amount of activity that had not slowed. Police officers and nursing staff milled around, intent on fulfilling their duties. Haley could see staff from the crime lab as well. "Joe? So much activity!"

"There is. It's a large crime scene." He touched her arm, pointing away from most of the activity. "Cayce is down this way. Let's get you to your fellow."

Haley's mouth opened to protest that he wasn't her fellow but she snapped it closed. Cayce was her fellow, her right hand finding the ring that he had placed on her ring finger. She sighed. This was supposed to be a happy time for her but it wasn't. Cayce had been hurt and now she didn't know if he was safe.

Joe paused for a moment, a hand on his temple once more. His head was pounding and he knew that he had to leave soon, as he had been directed to. His hand then rested on the door to a room before he shoved it opened. Joe nodded at the officer standing on guard before his hand was on Haley's back, shoving her into the room and allowing the door to close behind her.

Haley turned back to stare at the closed door, hesitating before she turned back to face the room. Cayce was watching her, his hand outstretched for her. She ran towards him, carefully throwing herself into his arms, feeling his wrapping around her.

Cayce held onto his lady as tightly as he could, grimacing with pain for a moment. He had no idea what had happened, awakening in a new room and being told that he was under police guard.

"Haley? Sweetheart?" Cayce waited almost impatiently for her to respond. "What happened?"

"I don't know. All I know is that this floor is a crime scene. That has to cause a horrible effort for the hospital to move everything around." Haley's head rested against his shoulder. "How are you? I think that you slept through all the excitement."

"No, I didn't sleep. I was told that I was given some sedation. We just don't know who did it or why." Cayce's anger grew at that. He was no longer the humble man who stood in the background. He was on the forefront of something that endangered himself and his sweetheart and his family. "I hear that Dad was knocked out as was Joe."

"They both were. Joe is around here somewhere even though he was told to go home." Haley stared at the door. "Can you leave, Cayce? Can you go home?"

"I can." Cayce bit at his lip for a moment. "Marry me, Haley. Marry me today."

"Cayce? We can't do that." Haley broke free from his arms and paced away, spinning to stand with her back to the door and staring at him. "We can't."

"We can, sweetheart. We can. Someone will get the license for us. We can be married at whatever home you want to. The minister is on board. He called a bit ago and I talked to him." Cayce sighed, his eyes closing. "I'm sorry. I'm rushing you. You need time to enjoy being engaged and then planning your wedding."

Haley stared at him and then up at the ceiling. She was torn, wanting to marry him but realizing that he was correct. They needed this time, to plan and even end this adventure that they were involved in.

Chapter 20

Haley stared down at the wood in front of her. A carving tool was clutched in her right hand but she was not working on the wood. Instead, her thoughts were on Cayce. He had been released and sent to his parents' home earlier that day, after he had pleaded with her to marry him once more. Haley didn't understand why he was asking that and she just couldn't say yes. She was a danger to him and his family. Yet, no one could tell her why she and Cayce were facing what they were.

Josh set a cup of coffee on the work table near his sister's arm and then laid a hand on her shoulder for a moment. He then wandered the room, a finger or hand out to touch his sister's wood crafts. Turning to study her, Josh drew in a deep sigh before he reached for the invoices for the orders that she had not had a chance to package and mail. He worked away in silence until he had the orders all caught up.

Haley looked up as she heard her father's voice, surprised to see the time. She had finally set aside her sober thoughts and become immersed in her work. Josh was sitting on the other side of the table, a book in front of him. He too looked up as his father came down the stairs.

"Dad? What's going on?" Josh shoved at the table, preparatory to rising but kept his seat as his father hugged Haley and then found a seat. Ben had a look on his face that said he was disturbed and was praying through what he had been told.

"Dad? You're troubled." Haley's hands were classed in front of her on the table. She waited patiently for her father to speak, knowing that he was working through what he needed to say.

"We need to pray, Haley, for both you and Cayce. I spoke with Joe earlier and he directed me to Isaac, who is investigating what happened at the hospital. They have no answers as to who or why. And that is worrisome because we have no idea how to protect you two." Ben studied Josh and then Haley. "Cayce called me."

"He did?" Haley sighed, holding out her hand. "I haven't had a chance to speak with you, Dad. We're engaged, in love, and trying to work that through with what we're going through." Haley blinked for a moment, her emotions almost overcoming her. "He wanted us to marry today."

"He did?" Josh shook his head. "And what did you say?"

"I didn't say anything. I ran. And I need to face that." Haley was sober. "How do we know how to proceed, Dad? How do we keep each other safe?"

"It's not your job to do that, Haley. God is in control and is well aware of what you are facing. You need to remember that He has walked this path before you. He sees the character of you both and has brought you two together. I have talked at length with Cayce over the last few days. He has a character that keeps him in the background, working to help other and to provide. He gives all glory to God. You are the same." Ben kept his eyes on his daughter, seeing Josh

———

watching her as well. "You are a team and a pair, Haley. Whenever it is that you decide to marry, it will be in God's timing. You ran today because you were scared. I wish your mother was here to talk with you. Seek counsel from Bessie and Anna. Skylor and Brynne would be good to speak to as well. There are others out there that Ardan assures me will speak with you who have gone through something like this." Ben hesitated before his hands reached out for those of his son and daughter. This was not surprising to the siblings. Their hands joined even as their heads bent for a time of prayer. This was how their family worked and had since Ben and his wife had married.

Haley walked rapidly up the stairs when their prayer time was finished. She needed some time alone, her right fingers twisting her ring. Haley needed to be with Cayce except he wasn't there. She reached for the phone that she had dropped on her bed and scrolled through her messages, her face softening as she read the words of welcome from Cayce's whole family and then the words of love from Cayce. Haley sank onto her bed, her head bent as she considered what she needed to do. Her thoughts were too muddled for her to think clearly through the process of what was needed.

Ben sighed before he followed Haley up the stairs, heading for the kitchen. He squinted at the clock as he reached for the meal in the oven and set it on hot pads on the table. None of them felt like eating, he was well aware, but they needed to.

Josh studied the packages that he had prepared and stuffed into totes ready to take to mail. He sighed as well before he was running up the stairs. He hesitated as he saw the meal on the table and then went to find Haley. He hesitated to disturb her but Haley was on her feet, heading into his brother hug and then walking past him. Josh turned to watch his sister, a feeling of sudden fear and terror washing through him. Haley was not done with whatever it was. He just prayed that it was over soon and that neither Haley or Cayce were harmed any further.

Cayce turned from the mirror in the ensuite in his bedroom at his parents' home. He was tired and hurt. A hand rested on his abdomen, feeling the bandages and then the pain from the stab wound. He had no idea who that man had been or even why it had happened. It also puzzled Cayce why he had been sedated earlier that day and then his father and Joe attacked. He could understand Joe but not his father. A sudden thought had him pausing. Was it about his father? Cayce's feet carried him towards his father's office.

Ardan turned as he heard rapid footsteps. A hand came out to stop Cayce's forward steps. He was shocked at the look of terror on his son's face. He shoved him into a chair and then drew one closer to his son's.

"Cayce? What is going on? What happened?" Ardan shifted on his chair to stare towards the door. No one other than he and Cayce were in the house. He knew that as Bessie had left with the girls. His other sons were meeting with an investigator. Anna had left, not saying where she was heading. She was heading for Haley to support that young lady.

"Dad? How sure are we that this is about me or Haley?" Cayce's words tumbled over themselves as he stuttered out his question.

"Cayce? What are you talking about?" Ardan was puzzled but was more worried at the whiteness of his son's face.

"What Haley and I are going through. What if it's not about us? What if it's about you?" Cayce slumped back in his chair, relieved that he had finally voiced his thoughts but more than a little troubled that he had questioned his father's life.

"Cayce? Are you saying what I think you're saying?" At Cayce's nod, Ardan buried his face in his hands. "I hear what you're saying, son. I have asked Simon and Blackie to look into some people. It's entirely possible that it is. Joe has asked me the same thing, just yesterday."

Cayce was relieved that his father had taken his words seriously. He just didn't know where to turn other than to God. God was in control, he acknowledged, and had a plan and purpose that he couldn't see at the present time and might never see.

Chapter 21

Ardan stared at his son, his mind whirling at Cayce's question. Was it about him or about Cayce? Or about Ben or Josh? Or none of them? Had Cayce been in the wrong place at the wrong time? Or was it about his business? Or his past work as a zoologist? Ardan had no answers for himself or his son.

"Why do you ask that, son?" Ardan waited patiently for Cayce to speak, knowing that his son thought through his words before he spoke. He had always been that way. Arlyn had been the most outspoken of the triplets, quick to speak his mind. Briar was a mix of his two brothers, sometimes quick to speak, sometimes taking time to think through his thoughts.

"I don't know, Dad." Cayce shrugged, praying that he might just be on the right track at last. He had to find out who was responsible and needed to do that to save his lady. His own life really didn't matter, he decided, but Haley's did. "I just don't understand any of this. Why attack you in the hospital and then attack Joe?" Cayce shrugged at his own words. "Joe? I can see. Take out the investigator and then bring in someone who would slow down or even stop the investigation. That would leave us in limbo for years, wouldn't it?"

"It would." Ardan studied the carpet under his feet, praying for the words that he needed. "I don't know that we have any answers to that."

"Can we meet with everyone this week? I heard from Blackie and Simon. They want to meet with us, just like they did with Arlyn and Briar. Abe and Emma are on board for that." Cayce slumped in his chair, sudden exhaustion hitting him.

Ardan was on his feet, drawing Cayce upright and then directing him to his bedroom. He watched carefully as Cayce was asleep almost before he laid down. Ardan's thoughts were highly troubled even as he prayed for God's protection on his son. Cayce was not one to ask for help, rather wanting to be the one who offered help. This time, it was different. This time, he was the one needing help. And no one could tell Ardan why. Ardan studied his son, seeing the whiteness of his face and the large dark circles under his eyes. When had he grown to be a man, he wondered? It seemed as if just yesterday the triplets were toddlers, into mischief and fun. Now, they were or had been in danger, even though they had met their life mates at the time.

Ardan walked away, his shoulders slumping, his feet almost too heavy to lift. He looked up as he sensed someone in front of him. He simply reached to wrap Bessie in his arms, holding his beloved wife as she wept for her son. This was taking a toll on all of the family. It had been bad enough with Arlyn but to have all three undergo this was almost more than they could bear in their humanness. God was providing the solace and strength that they all needed.

Bessie leaned back to look up at her husband, a frown on her face. Something had happened while she had been out.

———

"Ardan? What happened?"

Ardan hugged his wife. He had no words to tell her what he had to but he needed to.

"Cayce asked if this adventure that he and Haley are involved in was because of me." Ardan felt Bessie's arms tighten around him. "Bessie?"

"It could be. Did we ever look into that with Arlyn and Briar?"

"No, I don't know that we did. Someone else might have." Ardan swung Bessie around and headed for the kitchen.   He plugged in the kettle, needing a cup of tea to calm his nerves. Bessie moved around the kitchen as well, preparing a simple meal of sandwiches.

Their meal ended, Bessie stared at Ardan before she spoke.

"Where did he come up with that?"

"He's struggling to understand it all. We have little information to prove that it is him or that it is Haley. He wants to marry her, Bessie, but is hesitant to in case he brings more danger to her."

"I think Anna was heading towards Haley. I wish it was different, Ardan, but God is working through this all. I don't understand it all though." Bessie sat back in her chair, her eyes on the window across from her. "Was Cayce really serious?"

"He was. You know that he doesn't say anything that he doesn't mean and that he hasn't thought through. He's always been like that." Ardan sighed,

<hr>

his head resting in his hands. "How do we find out, love? How do we determine if he's correct or not?"

"We work with Joe or whoever it is." Bessie paused for a moment. "What if whoever it is thought that Joe was getting too close and took him out to prevent him from finding out the answers? And you were there, just as collateral damage?"

"That's possible. All we can do is pray for Cayce and Haley." Ardan looked around. "Where did Anna go to?"

Bessie shrugged, not sure how to answer her husband. What could she say or do, other than to bathe her son and his lady in her heartfelt earnest prayers? Bessie was known as the prayer warrior in the family, her prayers more than welcome with her family and friends.

"I don't know. She disappeared." Bessie bit at her lip. "I wonder if she went to find Haley. Haley needs a lady in her life right now. With what Anna went through, it would help Haley a lot to hear her story. Only, Anna never talks about her past."

"That's true. I often wonder what happened but she has never said. I catch a sadness in her eyes every once in a while with wistfulness on her face." Ardan never pried with what had happened to his sister. Anna would have told him had she wanted him to know.

"Me as well. The boys have often asked why she's so sad at times and withdrawn. It's not our story to tell, though." Bessie prayed for her sister-in-law, knowing that Anna would speak at some point. Or then again, she might not.

———

They both turned as they heard footsteps heading their way. Cayce appeared, slumping down into the chair that he preferred. Bessie was on her feet, preparing the bowl of soup and grilled cheese sandwich that he agreed to eat.

"Dad? What are your thoughts?" Cayce bit into his sandwich, the soup spoon held in his hand.

"About what you asked?" At Cayce's nod, Ardan shared a look with his wife. "I think that you might be on to something. There has always been something about what your brothers went through that didn't seem to finish. I pray that you are wrong."

"So do I, Dad, but I'm not sure that I am." Cayce's eyes slid shut for a moment as he tried to think of who it could be. "I heard from Blackie. They're heading this way in the next couple of days. I need to be at home. I have orders that I need to fill."

"You do but you also need to heal. Skylor and Brynne have both said that they plan on being with you tomorrow to help pack up what orders that you have ready to ship." Bessie walked away, tears brimming over from her eyes. She was just that distraught.

———

Chapter 22

Haley looked around the next day, her hand holding one of her carving tools. She had caught up on all her orders, thanks to Josh's help, and was working to craft more of her favourite animals and birds. She just didn't feel like working on them today but knew that the orders would still come in. Looking around as she heard the doorbell, Haley sighed and then dropped the carving tool on the work table. She headed for the front door, standing to one side to study who was out there. She didn't recognize the couple but she did recognize the tall handsome man who stood with them. Cayce had tracked her down, instead of working himself.

Opening the door, Haley stood with her hands on her hips, studying the man in front of her before he simply hugged her and then turned her to face the couple. No, she thought, not one couple but two.

"Haley, sweetheart, these are friends of ours. This is Blackie and his wife, Julia, and Simon and his wife, Eavan. They are here to discuss what they have discovered and what other friends have found and passed on to them. Let's find our places in your home. And I know that Simon wants to spend time in prayer before we go forward." Cayce felt Haley tensing under his arm and sighed. He had overstepped himself and opened his mouth to apologize.

"Don't you dare apologize, Cayce." The words were spit at him at Haley turned back to the house, the two ladies following her. She could hear snickers from the two men and bit back her own smile. The other two ladies were not so generous, their wide smiles showing their amusement.

Cayce's head dropped for a moment as he too struggled with his own laughter. A hand clapped his shoulder as Blackie followed the ladies, leaving Simon standing beside Cayce.

"She's a spitfire, Cayce. You didn't tell us that." Simon's amusement was evident in his voice.

Cayce shook his head, a laugh drawn from him.

"I didn't realize that she would react that way. I truly didn't." Cayce followed the others, Simon closing the door behind him.

An hour later, Simon looked around at the other five. He was hesitant to speak but knew that he had to. He locked eyes with Haley, finding her watching him in return.

"Haley? Talk to us. Tell us about your work and your website." Simon had a feeling that something was off somewhere.

"I don't know what to say, Simon. I don't have any enemies. If I have a competitor for my work, I am not aware of it. My website is maintained by Josh and he has a friend who searches for anyone hacking into it on a regular basis. He hasn't found anything yet." Haley's brow wrinkled for a moment. "I'm sorry. I just can't tell you what I think or what I know. There just isn't anything there other than a feeling that I am mixed up in something that I don't want to be involved in." She shifted on her chair to face Cayce. "Cayce had a thought that maybe it's about his father. Could it be about my father?"

"We've looked into that, Haley." Blackie spoke up this time. "We have some feelers out that may prove or disprove that fact." He handed over the folders that had rested on the table in front of him. "This is what we have found so far. Read through it and then call us." He rose as did the others. "We have a meeting that we need to get to. Call us, Cayce, Haley, at any time."

Haley watched as Cayce walked away with the two couples before she was on her feet, walking away from the table and the file that rested on the tabletop. She headed for her work bench, needing to lose herself in her work. Haley drew in a deep breath as she picked up her carving tool, hearing footsteps overhead and then Josh's voice. He was home already and shouldn't be.

Cayce searched the kitchen for Haley, not finding her. He didn't like to wander through her home, feeling himself as a visitor instead of her betrothed. Josh took pity on him and directed him to the stairs, watching in amusement as Cayce hesitated for a moment before he headed to find Haley.

Cayce wandered through her work room, a finger out to touch various wood crafts. She had a rare talent for carving he could see, similar to his own but in a different way. He turned at last to watch her, seeing the deep concentration on her face.

Haley looked up as she felt herself watched, her eyes stopping on Cayce. A frown covered her face.

"Cayce? What are your thoughts?" Haley didn't move from where she was seated. Her eyes dropped back to her work, not sure if he would ever reply.

"I don't know what to think, sweetheart. I truly don't. Blackie and Simon have verified what they told us and what they left for us. We'll need to go over it again with our families." Cayce found a stool beside her, his hand reaching for hers. "They have brought up some interesting points and comments."

"They have. I don't know what to think, either." Haley's eyes closed as she struggled with her emotions. She felt Cayce's arms come around her, felt his kiss on her forehead, and then heard his quietly spoken prayer just for her. She relaxed against him, cherishing the feeling of being loved by someone other than her family.

"It's okay, sweetheart. We'll figure it out. I suspect that Josh has read through the reports already. He pointed me this way before I came downstairs." Cayce refused to let go of his lady. "We'll get there, sweetheart. I promise you that. I just can't promise that we'll not be in danger again."

"Do you really think it goes back to your father?" Haley looked up at him, marvelling that such a handsome compassionate man had claimed her heart.

"I don't know, Haley. I truly don't. We'll need to work on that. For now, I need to let you get back to your work." Cayce bit at his lip for a moment. "You need to come and see my workshop. Maybe on Saturday? I don't use the whole shop and there is room to set up for you. I have a dedicated mailing area that has all the supplies that we would need." He reached to kiss her before he walked away, his steps sounding heavy and disheartened as he climbed the stairs.

Haley stared after him before she looked at the carving tool in her hand. A small smile broke out on her face. Only Cayce would hug and kiss her while she was holding something sharp.

Chapter 23

Sunday morning, Cayce stood in front of their church, arms folded across his chest. He was angry and knew that he had to release his anger. He just didn't want to. Cayce also knew that he was flanked by Arlyn and Briar as they all watched Joe walk towards them.

"The ladies are inside?" Briar looked around for a moment, before his gaze too went back to Joe.

"They are, or they're supposed to be." Arlyn sighed, knowing full well that Skylor, Brynne, and Haley were likely standing somewhere just behind them.

"They're not. They won't. They want to hear what Joe has to say." Cayce was convinced as well that the ladies were behind them, drawing curious and amused looks from the people entering the church. "Let's hope Mom and Dad and Aunt Anna are inside."

"We're not, son." Ardan appeared at Arlyn's side, knowing full well that the five ladies were lined up behind them.

"You're not?" Cayce leaned forward slightly, squinting against the bright sun. "Of course, you're not. Mom wouldn't let us be out here on our own, now would she?"

Ardan began to laugh, bringing smiles to his sons' faces.

"You know your mother all too well. And she's training your ladies, you do realize that, son?"

Briar sighed, agreeing with his father before he turned back to Joe.

Joe came to a halt in front of the five men. He looked up, seeking reassurance and answers from their God but none seemed to be forthcoming. Joe looked back at the four men and then the five ladies behind them. He smiled for a moment.

"Let's get through church first. Then, we meet. And I will tell you all that I know." Joe walked around them, leaving the men and most of the ladies shaking their heads.

Haley looked at him in disbelief even as she felt her brother's arm around her shoulder and sensed her father beside her.

"Joe's right, Haley. We do need to hear what is in the message this morning. Then, we'll meet. At our place, this time." Ben walked away from his daughter and son, leaving Haley feeling bereft. He knew that she was really missing her mother at this time but there was just nothing that he could do about that. He found his seat and then dropped his head to pray for his daughter and then for his son. Josh was hurting for his sister, Ben was well aware of that.

The service was just what the group needed. Haley snuggled under Cayce's arm as she listened intently to the message about being humble. She looked up at Cayce for a moment, seeing the intentness he had on his face as well. Haley didn't need to talk to him to know what he was thinking.

———

That afternoon, Ben turned to face all the people gathered in his home. His gaze sought out his daughter, worry in his eyes. There just didn't seem to be an end to how she was being threatened. There had been a threat tacked to their front door when they had returned from their church service. Joe had taken it, sealed it into an evidence bag, and then searched the area, finding nothing. He had asked about their security cameras which had been disabled. That frustrated both of them.

Joe stood beside Ben, searching the faces watching them. The group was quiet, the threat tamping down their conversation and spirits. He wished that it was different. He hurt that his friends were going through this. And Joe didn't have much information to give them. The assault on Ardan and himself was still unsolved. They had photos taken from the hospital security stream but there was not enough of the man's features showing to give them any idea of his face. Their feeling was that he was the same man who had posed as a nurse to sedate Cayce.

"Ben? Ardan? We need to spend some time in prayer." Anna spoke for the group before all heads bowed and they sought the peace, mercy, wisdom, and protection that only God could provide.

Ben looked around once more, focusing once more on his daughter and Cayce. He smiled to himself as he watched how carefully Cayce was treating Haley, wrapping her in his arms and holding her tight to himself without stepping over any lines. Ben appreciated that in the younger man, expecting nothing different from him.

———

"Joe? What can you tell us?" Cayce spoke up for the group, his eyes on Haley who had tilted her face up to study him.

"Unfortunately, not a lot. We just don't have that information or that tip that we need to solve this. The assailant at the hospital is still unknown. We don't have a picture that we can use to determine who it was." Joe was frustrated and it showed. "All we can do is ask that you two be as careful as you can be. This is far from over. Unfortunately, without any further information, we may have to set it to one side. And yes, Emma has been in touch. She indicated that she would be in touch with you and Haley this week, Cayce." Joe finally walked away, his head dropping as he stared at the ground. He had no idea who was behind all of this. Joe headed for his vehicle, stopping as he saw something white under the windshield washer. He looked around, not seeing anyone. Moving closer to the car, Joe's head tilted as he studied the envelope. His name was scrawled in black ink on the white envelope.

Joe reached for the envelope and opened it. He frowned. There was information here that they did not have but what the writer promised would help them. Joe had no idea who it was that had sent this but he would certainly be researching it. His head turned as he heard footsteps.

Cayce approached carefully, not sure what was going on with Joe. He stared at the paper in Joe's hand and then up at his friend.

"Joe? What's that?"

"This?" Joe held up the paper. "Someone left some information for me. I need to look into it." He squinted at Cayce. "How are you really doing, Cayce?"

Cayce shrugged. He had been asked that a lot that day by his concerned friends and fellow church goers.

"I don't know, Joe. I have no way to know how to feel. Do you?" Cayce didn't expect an answer. It was up to himself to decide how he felt and he just couldn't decide on that.

Chapter 24

Haley ran for her car through the pouring rain. She had dropped off orders at the local craft stores and then was heading for home. She stared out of the windshield, the wipers not really clearing the rain away. Haley sighed. She wasn't going anywhere right at the moment. She wiped at the steam on the window beside her and stared at the little cafe. Out of the car again, Haley ran towards the cafe, dodging the puddles as best as she could. This cafe would have to do for now until the rain slackened, if it ever did.

Slipping into a booth, Haley reached for the menu. She wasn't really hungry but she felt she couldn't just sit there without ordering something. Looking around, Haley nodded or smiled at those she recognized.

Joe hesitated as he stepped into the cafe, shaking off the rain as best as he could. He headed towards Haley, seeing her watching him. He sighed. This was not how he wanted to speak with her but speak with her he did need to.

"Haley? May I join you?" At Haley's nod, Joe slipped out of his jacket and then sat, nodding at the server as she held up the coffee pot. "You're in town?"

"I was. I had to drop off orders at the store and then the downpour kept me from driving home." Haley sipped at her cup of coffee. "You're on a break?"

"For now. I do need to talk to you." Joe stirred sugar into his coffee before placing the spoon on a napkin. "How are you doing?"

Haley shrugged. She searched the cafe, feeling watched but seeing only people from town.

"Someone's in here, Joe, watching us. Who is it? There are no strangers in here." Haley shivered in fear for a moment, totally unlike her.

"There is someone from town who is after you two. We just don't know why." Joe thought through the information that he could release. "I can't tell you who we suspect or why or even where the investigation is heading. You know that."

"I do, unfortunately. Skylor and Brynne have talked to me about it." Haley slumped back against the seat. "How do we stay safe, Joe? We can't hide. We have lives to live." She looked up as she sensed someone near her, her face lighting up as she recognized Cayce. He slipped down beside her, an arm around her as he kissed her cheek. "Cayce? Aren't you working?"

"I was doing some research at the library. The rain kept me from driving home." The town library was near the cafe. "I didn't expect to find you here. Or Joe either."

"I wasn't expecting to find either one of you." Joe looked around, sensing that they were safe to speak. "We do need to talk."

"Can we set it aside? I am tired of just talking with nothing happening." Haley glared at Joe for a moment, not backing down from him.

"Only for a while, Haley. We do need to go over some things." Joe hesitated. "Tell me, Cayce. What would it take for someone to use your crafts for nefarious purposes?"

Cayce nodded. Joe had asked the question that he had been asking himself.

"Like with Arlyn and Briar? My crafts are too small for that. It would be very obvious. I think that it is something else. And I think that it involves Dad. Don't ask me why I think that. I don't know nor do I have any proof of that." Cayce reached for Haley's hand, finding her fingers curling around his. "And have we considered that it might involve Ben or Josh?"

Joe nodded in turn.

"We have, Cayce, Haley. We are looking into your families and then reaching out to your relatives. Emma has some information that she is confirming. Then I understand that she and Abe are heading your way."

"Blackie and Simon left us some information but I don't know that it helps. Blackie was to forward a copy to you once he had confirmed more information." Cayce was at a loss. He was very worried about his family and Haley's family but even more worried about his lady. He watched as the lights from overhead glinted off her ring. "How do we do this, Joe?" Cayce's hand went up as Joe opened his mouth. "It's okay. I know that you can't tell us."

———

"No, I can't. Only God can give you that confidence in what you decide. And I know you both well enough to know that you are praying over your steps." Joe sighed as his phone chimed and he stood, reaching for his jacket. "Please, stay safe. I don't want to head to one of your families to let them know that you're dead." Joe walked away, leaving the couple staring after him before they stared at one another.

"What Joe said?" Haley leaned against Cayce, seeking strength from him. "Is that true?"

"About our families? They will look into them. That much I know. I don't think that they'll find anything." Cayce sighed, staring out at the teeming rain. "I don't know that the rain is stopping any time soon."

"No, it's not likely to. I need to go home but I can't drive in this." Haley shifted uneasily. "Someone is watching us."

"There is always someone watching us right now. I just wish I knew who it was. I'd confront them and stop this right now." Cayce was angry, justifiably so, he decided. Then, he shook his head. He needed to give that anger to God.

"We can't stay here forever, Cayce." Haley shoved at him, not finding him moving. "Cayce? We need to leave."

"We do. Leave your car here and come with me. I'll bring you back here. I'll be safe driving to my home but you can't drive home." Cayce was on his feet, paying for their meal, and then grasping Haley's hand tight in his as he ran for his truck and stuffed her into it. He then ran around the front of the truck to jump inside. "Do you want to go to my parents' home or mine?"

"Yours. We need to talk, Cayce, and make some decisions." Haley refused to look at him, her eyes on her ring.

"We do, sweetheart. We need to set a date for our wedding." Cayce drove carefully through the teeming rain, confident in his skills to transverse his way to his home. He shut the truck off once it was in the garage, watching the door close behind him. "Come on, sweetheart. Let's go through my home and see what you want to change. And you will make changes."

Haley nodded, soberness on her face. They did need to do that. She just wasn't totally convinced that they were making the right choice. God hadn't stopped their plans, so she knew that it was in His plans for them. She just didn't feel fully confident that they were following Him in this.

Cayce studied her before he wrapped her into his arms. He prayed for them as a couple and then for Haley as her own person. As she looked up at him when he finished, Cayce simply kissed her, sealing his love for her.

"God's here, sweetheart. He's in control. A friend says that God has a plan and purpose for us that we don't understand. Murphy is just so correct in that. We need to introduce you to Abe and Emma and Abe's security team." Cayce simply stood and held his lady, knowing that she needed to digest his words.

Chapter 25

Three weeks later, Cayce moved restlessly as he stood before the fireplace at Ben's home. Arlyn and Briar shared a quick grin before Arlyn's hand rested on Cayce's shoulder covered in his navy blue suit and prayed for his brother.

"She's not running away from you, Cayce." Briar grinned at his brother. "She wouldn't do that to you."

"I know. It's just everything that we're going through. I worry too much about her." Cayce continued to shift on his feet, not seeing the looks of sympathy directed his way. This was his and Haley's wedding day and their families and a few close friends were present. Joe was there, making sure that he had off-duty officers outside to protect the couple.

Haley stared at herself in her full-length mirror. Her mother's wedding dress, although slightly dated and yellowed to ivory, had fit her almost perfectly. She blinked back tears, wanting her mother there to share her day. Haley felt an arm around her and turned into her brother's hug.

Josh prayed for his sister, kissed her on her cheek, and then stepped backwards. Their relationship as siblings was changing, as it should. He was dating himself, a beautiful dark-haired beauty who completed his life. He nodded before he prayed for his sister and her chosen groom and then walked away, finding his girlfriend waiting to hug him in turn.

Ben stood for a moment, staring at his daughter. She was so much like her mother, he thought, so much like her mother on their own wedding day all those years ago. He too sorrowed that his wife was not there but he knew that God had planned this for his daughter. Ben just wished that the couple were not in danger. His feeling was that with their marrying, it would change the course of the danger and bring it to an even more intense level.

"Haley?" Ben's voice brought her head up and she turned to face him, the satin rustling quietly as she did so. "You are so beautiful, young lady. You are also almost the image of your mother on the day that we married." Ben reached to carefully hug his daughter, finding her clinging to him as she used to do when she was uncertain as a child. "Let me pray with you one more time as just my daughter. From now on, you are still my beloved little girl but you are now out on an adventure and life that God has set before you. Keep your eyes on God, Haley. Trust Him in everything. He has only the best in mind for you. He has already walked this path before you."

Haley was unable to speak, simply nodding as tears briefly filled her eyes. She clung to her father for a moment as he prayed for her before she stepped back and then reached to hug her father once more, kissing him on his cheek.

"Thank you, Dad, for being who you are. You stepped in when Mom died and raised Josh and me to be people who put God first. You have led by example. Your prayers have covered Josh and me in so many ways." Haley blinked. "Now, let's get this show on the road." She gave a quivering grin as he smiled at her words.

Late that afternoon, Cayce stared at the garage door that entered his home. He was now a married man, his bride in the truck beside him. He slipped from the truck and made his way around to open Haley's door. Cayce reached to kiss her before he gathered her into his arms, a small squeak coming from her. He grinned at her protest.

"I have to, sweetheart. I have to carry you into the house. It's what newlywed grooms do, you know." Cayce was as good as his word, his hip shutting the truck door before he headed into the house. He kissed Haley once more before setting her on her feet. "Okay, sweetheart?" He asked it hesitantly, not sure how to act now that they were married.

"I am, Cayce. You're not." Haley hugged him and then moved away, walking through the house that was now her home. "We'll get it all sorted out. We're leaving in the morning, right?"

"We are. I pray that we are safe but there are no guarantees that we will be." Cayce rubbed at the back of his neck. "We just have to place our hands in God's and trust Him."

Haley walked back to stand in front of him before she hugged him. Tears sparked in her eyes for a moment as she mulled over his words.

"That is so true, Cayce. It's hard to trust when there isn't something tangible that we can grasp on to. That's what faith is, isn't it?" She looked up to see him nodding.

"It is. We're told that faith is real but that it's the evidence of what we can't see. God has increased my faith in him through the last few months. It's been hard to see what Arlyn and Briar went through but even harder to see what you're facing." He sighed as he hugged her tighter, a kiss dropped to the top of her head. "Let's find our prayer corner, sweetheart, and spend some time before our Father."

A week later, Cayce walked through his home once more. There didn't seem to have been any disturbances. Joe had been through with his brothers, searching for anything that didn't belong. He had received a text from Joe that they hadn't found any cameras or anything that would track them. Cayce had stopped his steps abruptly as he read that. That had not even crossed his mind.

Turning as he felt a hand on his back, he swept Haley to his heart, kissing her before he looked around. He then led her to the back door and out of it, heading for his work building. Once instead, Cayce reached to flip on the lights and then watched as Haley moved around the building.

"Can you work here, sweetheart?" Cayce was so afraid that she wouldn't be able to and that her business would suffer.

"I can. It's so bright compared to the basement at Dad's. And you have it so organized." Haley spun in a circle, taking in his section of the building and then what they had set up for her. "And with a dedicated area for mailing, that makes a big difference." Haley had a huge grin on her face. "Now, about our websites. We need to link them."

"We do." Cayce's face suddenly paled and he staggered for a moment, catching Haley off guard.

"Cayce? Cayce? What happened?" Haley almost ran to him, her arms around him to steady him.

"Our websites. We need to have someone look at them. What if someone is hacking them and sending out wrong information?" Cayce's face paled even further as he saw the horror on her face.

"Do you think that?" Haley had never thought of that.

"I do. I have a friend who can do that. Let me send off a text to Noach. He's an ethical hacker and will look into it for us." Cayce turned to his work, seeing the orders that someone had printed for him. "We have a lot to do to get caught up in the meanwhile."

"We do. And the ladies are going to want to help." Haley moved away from him, intent on her own orders. She paused as she stared at the bottom one. "Cayce?"

Something in Haley's tone of voice raised Cayce's head from his work and brought him to her side.

"Haley?" His gaze followed her shaking finger to the piece of paper. "What? Let me send a picture of that over to Joe. Someone is playing with us and it's not our family. I can guarantee that. I wonder who all has been in here." He sent off a quick text to Arlyn who replied that some friends had dropped in while they were moving in Haley's belongings. He provided the names to Cayce, who frowned and then sent that text off to Joe as well. Someone was targeting one of them and they had no idea who or why as of yet.

Chapter 26

Joe looked down at the paperwork on his desk. He had too many investigators on the go and now that Cayce and Haley were back, he suspected that their case would heat up as they were wont to say. He didn't like that thought. His phone was out as he read Cayce's messages and frowned deeper. This was not what anyone of them wanted to hear.

Cayce turned from their front door and walked towards the kitchen. It was suppertime and they had enough to share with Joe. Joe quietly shut the door behind him and toed off his shoes, setting them tidily to one side with his jacket hung in the closet. He followed Cayce, stopping to hug Haley as she turned from setting bowls of chili on the table.

"You're welcome to join us, Joe. You've not eaten yet?" As he shook his head, Haley pointed to a chair. "Join us then for a meal. Set aside whatever it is that has you worried for an hour or two. Just relax if that's possible." She grinned as he grinned at her words.

"Thank you, Haley. It will be good to set everything aside for a while. I'm off duty now for a couple of days. I need that time." Joe bent his head as Cayce prayed for their meal and then was grateful for the prayer that his friend offered for himself. He needed those prayers each day, some days more than others.

Conversation was lighthearted, with Joe asking questions about their work and then about how the area had been that they had chosen for their honeymoon.

"It was wonderful. The cabin was in the woods, surrounded by towering pine trees and other trees." Haley smiled as she remembered the location. "We want to go back there in the summer. It is such a relaxing, refreshing area." Haley shared a look with Joe. "Joe, you need to go there. You need some time alone with God without having to worry about all these investigations. We'll give you that information and you need to do what we ask." Haley grinned at him.

Joe grinned back at her and then nodded.

"That sounds like a plan, Haley. I need to get away just as Jesus did, to spend time in solitude to get back to where I was." Joe looked down, his emotions overcoming him for a moment.

Their meal finished, Cayce sat once more, his hand reaching for Haley's. He knew that Joe was here for more than just to share a meal with them.

"Joe? You're here for a reason. What is it?" Cayce waited patiently for his friend to gather his thoughts and shift mode from friend to investigator.

"I am, Cayce. Haley, that order? Did it come through your website?" Joe watched her carefully, assessing her mood and trying to determine her thoughts. He could hear the grandfather clock in the living room striking the hour even as he waited.

"No, I don't think that it did. The letterhead was off. Someone made it up. I don't do those kinds of

———

crafts that they asked for. It is obvious from my website that I don't do crafts that would have a hollow centre. They are just too small for that. To try and put in a hollow would not give the structure that is needed to keep the craft in one piece." Haley bit at her lip. "Who did it?"

"That we don't know yet, Haley. We are looking at the friends who were here and then the investigation will spread from them outwards."

"Like a ripple in a pond from a thrown stone." Cayce nodded. "I see that. It's what you do." He waited for a moment, trying to gather his thoughts. "We have asked Noah to look at our websites."

"Noah?" Joe nodded. He knew that man and what he did. "That's a good idea. He'll determine if someone has hacked into your sites but knowing you both, you'll have them as tight as you can."

"We do, but the possibility is always there that someone can." Cayce sighed. "How do we do this, Joe? We can't continue for months under stress and fear. We have our lives to live. And we want to do that without bringing any danger to our families and friends."

"We know that you want to move forward in your lives." Joe sat back, his eyes on the framed winter picture on the wall across from him. He liked the faint yellow of the walls. It was relaxing. "We don't have enough information to move forward, Cayce, to determine who is behind this. You know that we are looking at everyone and everything."

"We know, Joe. It's just hard not knowing and trying to trust in God at the same time." Haley was on her feet, moving away from the kitchen, and then returning with a folder in her hands. "Take this with you. It's information that I've gathered from my orders in the last couple of years and also from Cayce's. It may not help but we had to do something to help."

"I'll take a look at it. For now, let me pray with you two, and then I'm on my way." Joe walked away at last, not comfortable leaving the couple on their own but he had no reason not to. That frustrated him greatly.

Haley worked at clearing away the remnants of their meal and setting away the leftovers. Cayce had disappeared into the office and she could hear him softly singing one of his favourite hymns. She smiled, happy to be married and to have Cayce as her beloved groom. Haley's thoughts sobered as she thought through the future and the possibilities, real and imagined, that they were facing. She prayed for him and then for their families. Sunday was to be the first meal that they would be together with their families since their marriage. She was uncertain of that, not wanting to bring any danger to them.

Cayce paused for a moment to study his bride. Love for her just kept growing in his heart. Unfortunately, his fear and terror for her was also growing. All he could do was pray for her and for the situation that they were in. Cayce fully trusted God in this, seeing what his brothers had gone through and what their friends had faced as well. He stared down at the small box in his hand before he walked towards Haley.

"Haley? Sweetheart?" Cayce hugged her before he stepped back. "Mom left this for me. It was her mother's and was to go to my bride. Gran did that for each of us." He opened the box to show a gold necklace with a small ruby stone in a setting. "She had these made for each of us, each with a ruby but with different settings. I would be honoured if you would accept it. Gran would have loved you." His voice trembled with his emotions as he considered his well loved maternal grandmother.

"Oh, Cayce! She thought that far ahead?" Haley hugged him once more and then turned to let him fasten the necklace. "Your family has proven how God works in them and through them. A ruby for a lady."

"That's right. Gran always told us that if we found the life mate that God had for us, we would find someone whose price was far above rubies."

Chapter 27

Three weeks later, Cayce walked towards his work building, lost in thought. He shook his head as he realized that time was flying and that they were no closer to ending this adventure. He wanted it over. And Cayce was well aware that Haley did as well. She had been very vocal about that not that long ago. In fact, he had had to walk away for a moment to get his composure back.

Haley looked up from her work to watch Cayce sit at his table and then focused once more on the wood that she had been turning over and over. She didn't feel like working that day and she didn't think that Cayce did either. However, the waiting orders meant that they had to work on their crafts.

Cayce sighed at last, dropping his tools and rising to walk over to Haley. He waited until she paused her work and looked up at him. He simply wrapped her into a hug, feeling her hugging him back.

"We need a break, sweetheart. I'm taking you out for lunch." Cayce reached for her hand, locking the building behind them, and heading for his truck. "Where to?"

"I have no idea." Haley blew out a breath. "When is this going to be over, Cayce? I am tired of watching everywhere we step, just in case we put someone in danger. Do you know that?" She glared at him as his grin widened as her words continued. "It's not funny, buster."

Cayce could not hold back his laughter. His eyes gleamed with his amusement as she continued to glare at him even though her own eyes sparkled with laughter.

"You're so good for me, sweetheart. You're bringing fun and love into my life."

"As well as danger." Haley moved into his hug before she reached for her jacket and shoes. "Wasn't something said about a meal?" She opened the front door to stop short.

Cayce stopped abruptly as well, staring at the men who stood there. His hand drew Haley back into the house quickly and slammed and locked the door. His phone was out calling for emergency help. Cayce just didn't know if they would reach them in time.

Haley spun, trying to determine the best place to hide before Cayce grabbed her hand and ran for the master bedroom. He slid back the access panel to the attic and lifted her through.

Haley watched as he jumped for the opening, his hands and arms pulling him through before the access panel was shoved back into place and wooden buttons turned over it to prevent it from being opened. Cayce's finger rested on her lips as they heard the crash of the front door broken open and then running footsteps and loud voices as the men searched for them. Cayce wrapped Haley into his arms, hiding her face against him. He had no idea if the men would search for the access to the attic.

Sirens sounded as the men still struggled to find them. The couple could hear louder voices and then the voices of the officers as the men were arrested. Haley's eyes were huge as she stared at Cayce.

Cayce reached for his phone, feeling the vibration as a call came in. He squinted at the number and then sent off a swift text.

Joe stared at the text and then looked around. Haley and Cayce were safe for now, hidden away as they were in the attic. He would leave them there for now.

An hour later, Joe stared up at the attic access hole. He had texted Cayce to come down but Cayce just wasn't doing that. Joe texted him again and then heard the access panel slowly moving to one side.

Cayce peered down at Joe, Haley peeking over his shoulder.

"Is it safe?" Haley's voice was a whisper, almost as if she was afraid that Joe wasn't Joe.

"It is." Joe grinned up at them. "How be you come down and we talk?"

Cayce turned his head to study his bride, finding her studying him in return. She shrugged as if to say why not.

Cayce swung himself down and then reached to catch Haley around the waist as she wriggled to come down feet first. He hugged her while looking at Joe over her head.

"Who were they, Joe?" Haley spun in Cayce's arms to face the investigator.

"We don't know as yet. But we do know that they meant you harm. You would have died, both of you, had you not hidden yourselves away." Joe's face was as grim as his words.

Haley gave a small cry and then spun to bury her face again her groom, her sobs sounding in the room. Cayce's face tightened with both worry and anger. They had been that close to dying that day.

"What do we do, Joe? They've invaded our home. We can't just pick up and leave it. We have our work that we need to do and we can't do that just anywhere." Cayce spit his words at Joe, who was nodding.

"We know that, Cayce. We are well aware of it. For now, we have officers who are volunteering to be around here on their time and days off." Joe's hand went up at the protest from both Cayce and Haley. "We are doing this to try and keep you two alive. Today proves that someone wants the worse for you." He walked away after haring what they had to say.

"Did he really just do that?" Haley frowned after him as she followed him to the door.

"He did, sweetheart. He's heading to the detachment to hear what the men have to say. I could almost guarantee that he won't find out anything from them." Cayce stared past Haley. "Come on back in, sweetheart. We need to figure this out." He drew her back into the house and wrapped her into his arms. "I love you, sweetheart. I was so afraid that we wouldn't find somewhere to hide."

"I love you too." Haley reached to kiss him. "Would they have found us?"

"It's hard to say. They might have." Cayce didn't express what he had feared, that they would have been found and that shots would have be fired into the attic when access was denied to the men.

"I think that they would have. And we wouldn't be having this conversation right now." Haley shuddered with fear. "Why? We seem to be asking that without any answers. We need to set up a family meeting, Cayce, and soon."

"We will. Mom wants us to come for lunch on Saturday. I'll send word to everyone that we need to work this. Blackie and Simon will be there as will Noah and his wife, Rowan. Abe and Emma are planning on it as well. We'll see how we move things forward at that point."

Chapter 28

Ardan's keen eyes studied first his son and then his son's bride on the Saturday afternoon. They had gathered for lunch, Ben and Josh included as they were now considered family. He shook his head. Something had happened that the couple had not shared with their family. Whatever it was had scared his son and that took a lot.

Abe stood beside Ardan, his own eyes studying his friends. He knew that Emma had information for them. Emma had a business where she found people and information that no one else could find. She had been working hard to determine who was at fault and just didn't have enough information to concretely state the name.

"Abe? What happened to them?" Briar stood beside his friend, watching the activity around them.

"I don't know but they're scared." Abe had seen it far too often in his work with his security team. He also knew that the other seven members of his team were outside and around town, trying to determine how best to keep this couple safe.

"They are." Arlyn spoke up.

"Something happened the other day that terrified Haley. She just won't say what." Josh knew that his sister was hiding something and he hated that. He wanted her to be open with him but she wasn't. Not any more.

"There was." Joe appeared in front of them. "They'll speak about it today. I won't let them get away with not telling you. What happened to them could have had dire consequences." Joe walked away to find Cayce, dragging him back into the house and to his family. "Cayce, we're ready to meet and you need to be open with your family."

"I know, Joe. It doesn't mean that I want to." Cayce was distraught and trying hard to hide it. "It's going to devastate them, knowing how close we were to death."

Joe looked past Cayce to see Anna standing there, her hands over her mouth, shock on her face. The cat was out of the bag, he decided, but he also knew that Anna would not say anything until Cayce did. She walked away, struggling with her emotions.

"We'll spend some time in prayer first, Cayce. Then, you and Haley need to talk. It's not fair or safe to keep this quiet."

"We know that, Joe. It's just hard to have to admit that we were so close. Haley hasn't been sleeping properly and I must say, I haven't either. We want this over but it just keeps dragging on." Cayce walked away at that point to find his bride, leaving Joe turning to find Blackie, Simon, and Noah standing nearby.

"Joe? Is what he said true?" Simon spoke at last. He was an ex-cop and ex-military police officer, now working as a private investigator. Nothing surprised him any more.

———

151

Joe sighed. He couldn't keep this from his friends or Cayce's friends. He just nodded silently, leaving the three other men to share looks.

"Then, we have a lot of work to do, don't we?" Noah walked away to find Josh and Briar, needing to ask them some questions that he wasn't sure they could or would even answer.

"We do. And it's not going to get any easier or safer for them." Blackie as he was called, only his mother using his proper name of Levi, knew as well as Simon what the couple were facing. He had faced danger with his wife, Julia, just after they met.

Raising their heads at last after a long and intense session of prayer, Cayce wrapped Haley as tight to him as he could. She didn't mind. She could feel his strength and sense his strong desire to keep her safe.

"Okay, Joe. You start. What can you tell us?" Cayce spoke for the group, the others waiting for Joe to answer.

Joe stared at the couple, turning over in his mind what he could tell them. There was not a lot, unfortunately.

"We know the names of the men. They are from out of town, that much I can tell you. We haven't been able to track down, however, who has employed them. They are wanted in many municipalities. They will need to be transferred across the province to face murder charges." Joe's hand went up as Haley protested at that. "That's what happens, Haley. We are working on the charges here but the older and more serious charges take precedence over ours. We won't forget them."

"What else, Joe?" Ardan spoke up, his eyes moving between his three sons. He could see how this latest adventure or whatever it was had affected the brothers.

"Not a lot. We're working through what we have, reaching out to other forces, searching for that one lead that will break this open. We just don't have it yet."

Emma spoke at last, detailing what she had discovered. The group was shaking their heads at what she had found, not really believing her but knowing that she spoke the truth.

"Do you really think it goes back that far, Emma?" Briar's hand tightened on Brynne's.

"I do. I have evidence of that. Cayce, I'm sorry. I prayed that it wouldn't be that way but it is. Ardan? Ben? Did you know that your great-grandfathers were friends and business partners?" Emma's question took the two older men by surprise.

"I didn't know that." Ben shared a look with Ardan. "What business? I have forgotten what he did."

"They were importers of food from overseas. They had a nice little niche business on the go but then your grandfather died, Ardan, and that ended the business. Your grandfather moved from here, Ben, but his son returned to try and make a living as a farmer. He did that. Your fathers were acquaintances, not knowing the history of what business their grandfathers shared. You have a connection there that was unknown to a lot of people." Emma shuffled through her papers. "Joe, I have a file full of this information for you with any and all names that you should need. Jace and Naomi have verified everything that is in there. If you have questions, talk to them, not me. It's how we work. Whoever finds and verifies the information is who you speak with. That way, nothing is lost."

"Thank you, Emma. Our team will reach out to them." Joe flipped through the folder, nodding as he saw the myriad of information that was there. "This will certainly help."

The three brothers had been sharing looks, Simon and Blackie watching them closely.

"What are you thinking, guys?" Simon spoke for the group.

"We don't know, Simon. This is something that we need to digest and discuss." Briar shifted on his chair, Brynne's arm around him. "Where do we go from here? Noah? You've looked at all of our websites?"

"I have. So far, I haven't been able to find any evidence that someone has been able to hack into them. You have good security set up on them. I'll keep a watch on them." Noah shared a look with Rowan. "What else can we do for you two?"

Haley shrugged before she had a thought. She didn't know how Cayce would feel about it but they had to do something.

———

154

"We need to go on the offensive. We can't continue as we are. They'll just continue to up their game until we're dead." Haley was sober as she spoke. Cayce's arm tightened around her as he faced the group.

"I agree with Haley. We need to do something. If we don't, this will continue to escalate and go on for months." Cayce caught the nod that Abe was giving. "Abe? You have some ideas."

"My team is working on some as are two other teams who are good friends of ours. Let us work through this and then we'll meet again. For now, let's spend some more time in prayer and then we have to get on the road." Abe was as good as his word, bowing his head to pray for the couple.

Chapter 29

A week later, Cayce turned from the living room window. It was night and he was uneasy. There had been no further attempts to kidnap them or kill them. That thought always caused him to whiten and his thoughts would grow dark. Cayce could hear Haley quietly singing to herself as she cleaned the kitchen after their meal. He had offered to help but she had kissed him and sent him out of her way. His head tilted as he listened to what she was singing and smiled. Her songs were the old hymns that mentioned the blood of Christ. He was well aware that without God, they would likely be dead by now. That terrified him. Cayce felt as if what he and Haley were facing was much worse than what his brothers faced, not to say that what they had faced was anything less.

Haley paused as she swiped at the sink with the dish cloth, her singing pausing for a moment. She was happy, she decided, being loved and loving in return. Cayce was just who she needed and who she knew that her father had prayed for. Haley dropped the dish cloth and turned to find Cayce standing behind her.

"Haley? What are you thinking? I know that you're plotting something." Cayce grinned as she shook a finger at him.

"I think we need to be out and about more. The weather is starting to get warmer. It's March, after all, in Southern Ontario. How do we do that?" Haley hugged him and then spun away from him. Her mood seemed more upbeat as she did so.

"Haley? Are you sure?" Cayce grinned as she enthusiastically nodded. "Okay. That's what we do. We work until late afternoon." He bit at his lip. "We're busy enough that we need someone to take over the orders and mailing."

"I know that we are. Skylor and Brynne want to help. So do your Mom and Aunt Anna." Haley was happy that night, happier than she thought that she had ever been.

"They have? They did that with Briar as well. We'll work with that for now. At some point, we'll hire someone. I don't want to bring someone else into the mix at this point." Cayce hugged Haley close before he thoroughly kissed her. "It's Friday tomorrow. Let's finish our work early and then I am taking my bride out for a meal."

"You are, are you?" Haley grinned at him. "And does your bride agree?"

"She does. Let's find our prayer corner, Haley, and spend time before our Father. We need the protection and strength that only He can bring." Cayce led her to the corner of the office where Haley had settled two upholstered chairs and a small table. His Bible lay on it from when they had done their Bible study that morning. He seated her, sat himself, and then reached for her hands. Both of them realized that it was only God who would get them through the next few days and weeks. They both prayed that their plan would bring their adventure to a quick and final end.

Late Friday afternoon, Cayce reached for Haley's hand as they walked towards a popular Italian restaurant. He was dressed up in a suit and tie and Haley had taken the time to dress up in a soft jade dress, low heels, and a shawl. He smiled to himself. She had been so uncertain as she had approached him, not confident in how she looked as she was dressed up. Cayce had hugged her and then kissed her before telling her how beautiful she was, something that she denied even with a pleased look on her face.

With their meal completed, Cayce drew Haley towards the walkway along the river. He was in no hurry to head home, content to be out with his lady. He shivered for a moment, feeling evil near them and not knowing who it was. No one had yet been able to confirm a name or even a reason.

"Cayce? Are we safe enough out here?" Haley was searching for someone or something. She wasn't sure which that she should be looking for.

"We should be. We have to live our lives regardless of the danger. You've talked to a lot of the ladies of friends."

"I have." Haley sighed. "I didn't know so many went through this. They have been a great source of information and advice." She looked down at the river, her hands grasping the iron railing. "I just want this over, Cayce."

"So do I." Cayce turned to face the trees and gardens behind them. "We need to think about what we want to do outside of our home. I just didn't do anything even though Mom and Aunt Anna tried to get me to change the gardens."

"I can do that. I worked on ours." Haley drew in a deep breath. "We need a pet."

"We do, do we?" Cayce grinned at her. "Dog or cat?"

"Both. You need a dog. I need a cat." She grinned up at him. "Josh found a small calico kitten last night. He doesn't want her and offered her to me."

"A calico? Do you how crazy they are?"

"I do. I've always wanted one." She turned as well, tugging him with her as she walked back towards his truck.

"Well, then, I guess that we have a kitten." Cayce hesitated before he drove away, seeing lights in his rearview mirror. "Make sure that your seatbelt is buckled. I have a bad feeling."

Haley shifted on the seat, staring through the back window.

"They're following us, sweetheart. Pray that we are able to get home safely and lock ourselves away safely." Cayce drove as swiftly as he could and soon had the garage door locked behind them.

Haley paced the house early the next morning. She was highly troubled, her phone dinging multiple times over night with the threats. She had finally risen, leaving Cayce still sound asleep. Troubled about the text messages, Haley had finally forwarded them on to Joe. She was still waiting for him to respond. And then Haley remembered that he was away for the weekend. That didn't help her out at all.

Cayce rolled over in bed, reaching for Haley. Not finding her still asleep, he rose, dressed, and searched for her. She was standing at the back door, staring out into the dimness, no lights on in the kitchen. Haley jumped as he moved in to wrap her in his arms.

"Can't sleep?" Cayce's voice still had that early morning drawl.

"No. My phone kept going off all night with horrible text messages. I sent them on to Joe but he's away until Monday." Haley was sober as she spoke, not looking up at him.

"That's okay. Abe said to send anything to him as well. His team is willing to take a look at them. One of his team members, Micah, is their computer whiz and may be able to trace them." Cayce rested his chin on the top of her head. "We have to do some shopping today."

"We do?" Haley searched her mind for what they needed to buy.

"We do. We need to find a pet store and get what we need for your kitten." Cayce felt Haley relax against him.

"We do, don't we?" Haley spun and hugged him. "Are you sure?"

"I am. If it makes you happy and content, then yes. We'll look at dogs next. That will take some research." Cayce grinned down at her. "Why do I think you already have a breed in mind."

"I do. A Shetland Sheepdog. They are a wonderful breed, small but feisty, and very family oriented." Haley reached to accept his kiss. "It's so early, Cayce."

"It is. Let's take our office and find our prayer corner. I sense that we are coming into the most dangerous part of our adventure."

Chapter 30

Two weeks later, Haley turned from the back yard and walked towards their work building. She had been taking a break from her work and decided to walk through their yard with an eye to what she wanted to change. Haley didn't hear the footsteps that raced towards her until arms came around her and trapped hers to her side. A hand was clapped across her mouth, stifling her scream. She twisted and turned in her attempts to escape but was unable to.

The men surrounding her didn't move, staring around before the man holding Haley bodily carried her towards the work building. There were whispers among the men, too low for Haley to know what they were saying.

Cayce was on his feet, shocked and horrified as the building door flew open and slammed into the wall. His startled and then angry eyes fastened on the man holding Haley who was continuing to struggle.

"Let her go!" Cayce moved to stomp towards the man, sliding to a halt as a weapon was trained on Haley. "Put that away! What do you want?"

"We want you." The man holding the weapon now trained it on Cayce. "You two are coming with us."

"Not a chance!" Cayce was adamant that he was not going with the man. "Let her go!"

The man holding Haley gave a startled yell and dropped Haley to the building cement floor. She scrambled away from him and then ran for Cayce, finding his arm out to wrap her close to his side. His eyes didn't move from the man who was holding the weapon on them.

The men grew restless as the standoff continued. Cayce refused to move and kept Haley tight to him. The man holding the weapon inched his way towards the couple, two of the other men moving with him. One of the men stood at the open door, on guard for anyone approaching them. There was silence outside the building except for the sounds of nature and the sounds of traffic on the surrounding streets.

The man, an older man with straggly hair and beard, finally just reached for Haley and tore her from Cayce's arms. Cayce lunged for her, but the weapon descended on his head and sent him to the floor where he lay still for a moment.

Haley's scream split the air and her hands flailed at the man, hitting him the face and eyes. A cry came from the man as his hold on Haley loosened. She tore herself from him and then fled towards Cayce, on her knees in her attempt to turn him over.

Cayce roused slowly, hearing Haley's cries for him to wake up and then the commotion around him. He sat up, a hand to his head, Haley's arms around him holding him upright. Haley's eyes were on the four men, watching as they huddled together near the door, angry glares sent their way. She was terrified, afraid that they would die or else disappear forever.

Cayce shifted so that he could wrap an arm around Haley. He had no idea who these men were or what they wanted. All he knew was that they had manhandled his bride and that wasn't something that he would accept. He felt Haley's arms tighten around him as she bent closer to his ear.

"I don't know who they are. They just appeared in the yard. I didn't hear them at all until that man grabbed me." Haley kept her eyes on the man who had assaulted her.

"No, I don't think that I know who they are either." Cayce was trying desperately to come up with a plan but no plan was coming to him. "We need to get away."

"I know, but I don't know that we can." Haley looked around before her eyes went back to the men. "If we can get the door out to the reception area closed and locked, we may be able to hide."

"I don't know if we can do that. They're watching us too closely." Cayce carefully climbed to his feet, drawing Haley with him. That movement brought all eyes to them before the men went back to whatever it was that they were discussing.

"How do we do this, Cayce?" Haley's lips were barely moving even as she searched for a way to escape. "Can we do that? Lock the door?"

"I'm not sure that we can make it over there without them coming this way." Cayce watched as Haley shook her head and then moved away from him, heading for her work bench that sat closest to the door.

The men watched Haley for a moment before going back to their discussion which was now becoming more and more heated. They were then ignoring the couple.

Haley kept an eye on the men even as she moved closer to the door, picking up and setting down objects on her work table. At last, she was close enough to the door. Haley glanced back at Cayce, finding him shaking his head at her. She shrugged and then leapt for the door, slamming it and shoving the dead bolts on. It was a steel door and would be very difficult for the men to break down.

Cayce ran for her and reached for her hand, pulling her with him. His eyes were searching for a place to either escape or hide. Haley pulled at him and pointed towards a hidden alcove in the corner. He pulled her that way and tucked her into the corner, pulling boxes in front of her and then squeezing in beside her. Cayce wrapped in his arms and tried hard to control his ragged breathing. Haley hid her head against him, trying to control her own breathing. She could hear Cayce's softly whispered prayer for protection.

There was loud hammering at the door before one of the men ran outside and around the building to try the windows and the other door. He was not able to get inside. Back with the others, there was a lot of angry yelling and blaming of each other. They were so wrapped up in blaming each other that they didn't hear the sounds of footsteps running their way.

Joe had approached Cayce's home not that long earlier. He had frowned at the van sitting haphazardly in the driveway and quickly called in the plate. He had then asked for officers to respond but not to use sirens or lights.

The officers moved in quietly, Joe in the lead, as the men spilled out of the building, arguing among themselves. The men had been shocked, to say the least, to find themselves arrested. Joe watched them led away before he entered the building and then tried the door. He nodded. Somehow, Cayce and Haley had managed to lock themselves into the larger part of the building. He just needed them to open the door for him.

Cayce pulled out his phone, reading the text message. Haley leaned against him, reading it as well.

"How do we know it's Joe?"

"It's his phone number." Cayce grinned down at Haley.

"It can be spoofed. Tell him to prove it's him." Haley was adamant on that. She refused to back down from Cayce despite the incredulous look that he gave her.

"Are you serious?" Cayce sighed as Haley vigorously nodded. "Okay, but you get to explain to him why."

"He'll know why when he receives your text." Haley slumped against him, her legs shaking as her fear and adrenalin released.

Chapter 31

Staring at his text message from Cayce, Joe shook his head even as a smile cracked through the grimness of his face. He tilted his phone to show the officer beside him who laughed hard at the request.

"Guess you have to do that, Joe. They're not coming out otherwise." The officer continued to laugh. "Can't say as I blame them."

A huge grin was on Joe's face as he took a picture of himself and the officer and sent it to Cayce.

"That would be Haley asking that. She's smart, you know." Joe heard the sound of running footsteps and then the door to the work room was unlocked to show Haley standing there, a frown on her face as she stared at him.

"It is you. Good. Now, where are those men?"

"They're gone. We've arrested them. Can't you two stay out of trouble?" Joe grinned at Cayce who was grinning in response.

"We're not getting into trouble. It's everyone else who's causing it." Haley leaned back against Cayce. "Can we go to the house?"

"Sure. Head that way. And don't talk to anyone. This building is now a crime scene. And I need to get your statements before you talk to anyone." Joe grinned again as he heard Haley grumbling under her breath. "What was that you said, Haley?"

______

Haley turned to glare at him, not seeing the smile that Cayce was also trying hard to hide.

"You don't want to know, Joe. You really don't want to know." She stalked away from them, heading for the house, an officer trailing behind her.

Cayce watched as she walked away before he too left the building. He stalked through the yard, trying to determine where the men came from. He moved around the officers searching as well, without determining that entry point. Cayce turned to stare at the house, seeing Haley standing on the back porch. He walked towards her, wrapping her into his arms before he began to pray for her.

"Where do we go from here, Cayce?" Haley whispered her question against Cayce.

"We go on with our lives. They are trying hard to kidnap us and force us into something. I just don't know what. I wish I did know. I would stop it today." Cayce knew that Joe had approached and was waiting to speak with them. "We can't hide. It doesn't seem to matter where we are. I just wish I understood what started all this." He turned his head to look at Joe. "Joe? Do you know?"

"Not really, Cayce. Whoever it is? They are being very careful. We have hints and tidbits of hints. We have arrested men who are refusing to speak, whether because they won't, are too afraid to, or just don't know the reason why. They're what we consider low men in the organization." Joe sighed. "I wish this was over too. I just don't know any more." He walked away, troubled about his friends and praying that he would soon solve this. That possibility seemed too far away for him to have any hope.

Haley watched him walk away before she hugged Cayce tighter and then moved out of his arms. She reached for her phone which had been chiming. Frowning at the message, Haley walked back into the house. She reached for the folder that Emma had left and then sat at the kitchen table, reading back through the information. A pen in her hand marked what she was discovering.

Cayce moved quietly around the kitchen, watching Haley even as he prepared a meal for them. He reached to shove the folder to one side despite her protest.

"We need to eat something, Haley. Just some soup and a sandwich." Cayce reached for her hands. "Let's eat and then pray. Then, I want to know what it is that you've discovered."

Haley shoved her bowl and plate aside and then wrapped her hands around her mug of coffee. She watched Cayce carefully, seeing the stress and strain that he was trying had to hide.

"Cayce? Where is God in all of this?"

"He's right here, sweetheart. He's walking beside us and has already gone before us. He's brought friends in to help us. He's not leaving us." Cayce reached to hug her before spending time in prayer. Sitting back, Cayce looked at the folder before he pulled it over and read through her notes. "You think this?"

"I do. I think he's the one behind this. How do we prove it?" Haley bit at her lip for a moment. "We're going to have to be out there, Cayce. We'll need to take extra care not to be harmed or kidnapped again. He's getting desperate, isn't he?"

"I know that we do, sweetheart." He hugged her tighter, his thoughts muddled. He was beginning to get flashes of what had happened to him, or at least what he thought had happened to him. He just wasn't sure if that was the truth or not.

"You're troubled, Cayce." Haley stepped away from him. "What can I do for you?"

"Nothing, sweetheart." Cayce squinted at the clock. "It's time to eat but I sure don't feel like it."

"I don't. I want to solve this and solve it now." Haley sighed as she finished her words. "That's not happening, is it?"

"Not tonight. Joe is working through what happened today. I was so afraid for you." Cayce wrapped her tight into a hug once more.

Haley nodded, afraid for her groom as well. There was no sign in sight for an end to what they were going through. They had discussed what they were facing many times. The couple had not been receiving the threats by text, voice mail, or by packages. That had surprised them.

Joe had nodded when they had talked to him about that. He was well aware that they were not getting what everyone else had received. That troubled him and the other investigators. They had all come to the conclusion that whoever it was? They were that close to the couple and also their families. The difficulty was deciding who it was and then arresting them.

Chapter 32

Early the next morning, Haley roused, her head coming up from the pillow. She had been deep in sleep but something had awakened her. She turned over to find Cayce's head tossing from side to side, his body jerking with his movements. Haley sat upright, a hand on her mouth to prevent her scream and then she reached for her groom. Her hand rested on his chest.

Cayce's movements stilled for a moment before he began to toss and turn. Haley's wrapped him into her arms, trying desperately to stop him but that didn't work. She listened carefully as he muttered, not sure what it was that he was saying but knowing that he was telling her who it was. Her face whitened as she caught the name. It couldn't be that person or couple, could it? Haley was sure that Cayce wouldn't remember who it was.

On her feet, Haley ran for the office, scrawling the names on a pad of paper. She stood and stared at the paper before dropping the pad of paper onto the desk top and then running back to the bedroom.

Cayce was sitting upright at that point, staring towards the window. Haley knelt on the bed beside him, wrapping her arms around him. She could feel the shudders that were shaking his body. Cayce just wasn't responding to her pleas and she had no idea what to do next.

Cayce's eyes slid closed as he collapsed back on the bed, taking Haley with him. His eyes closed and he slept, still moving restlessly. Haley lay motionless for a few moments, her eyes on the ceiling. She had no idea what had just happened, other than that Cayce was deeply disturbed by something. Her head turned on the pillow as she studied him, a frown crossing her face. She sighed and then began to pray for her groom. Only God could solve this mystery for them and bring them through without any more harm or hurt coming to them. Haley just didn't have enough faith to trust that this would happen. Her prayer changed to begging God for faith enough to trust Him.

On her feet a few hours later, Haley yawned as she stood at the kitchen counter. Joe had arrived, nodding at her before he reached to make coffee for them. He was wanting to talk to them both but Cayce hadn't appeared yet.

Haley handed him the paper that she had scrawled the names down on. She then reached for her mug of coffee and found a place to stand and stare out of the back door.

"What is this, Haley?" Joe didn't look at the paper at first, keeping his eyes on Haley.

"Cayce seemed to be having a nightmare last night or rather early this morning. He kept saying those names." Haley looked up, blinking back tears, begging God to end their adventure that day.

Joe looked at her once more and then glanced at the paper. His eyes stopped as he read the names.

"Haley? Do you know who these people are?" Joe shot her a surprised look.

Haley turned at the question in his voice. Her head nodded as she indicated that she knew who they were.

"I do. I just don't know why they would be after us." Haley knew full well who the couple were and what they were involved with in town. "There have always been rumours about their kids, just not them. What has Cayce discovered?"

"That we will need to ask him. Any chance that he's away?" Joe looked behind him towards the hallway.

"I'll go see. I can't promise anything, Joe." Haley walked away, leaving Joe staring at the names. She quietly opened the bedroom door to see Cayce heading her way. "You're awake!"

"I am." Cayce reached to hug her and then kissed her. "You've been up for a while."

"Yeah, about that." Haley shoved away from him and pointed towards the kitchen. "Joe's here."

"He is? That's early for him." Cayce narrowed his eyes as he studied his bride. "What happened?"

"You named some people early this morning. You were having nightmares. I couldn't awaken you, no matter what I tried." Haley was sober as she said that.

Cayce's eyes closed. He knew that he had been having nightmares. He just didn't think that he had woken Haley up with them.

"What happened, Haley?" His arms tightened around her.

"I couldn't get you to wake up. You kept saying the names of a couple and then two other names. I wrote them down." Haley looked up at him, a sober look on her face, fear in her eyes. "I know who they are."

"What names?" Cayce waited for Haley to speak. "Haley? What names did I say?" He had anger in his voice, not directed at her but at the situation.

Haley told them, her voice shaking as she did so. Cayce stared at her before his eyes closed. He had no memory of that but then his nightmares had scared him. Cayce had not realized that he had spoken any names. He was shocked that he had and had no idea why he had named them.

"Do you know them?" Haley stared at him before she glanced towards the doorway.

"I do. They wanted to invest in my company but I refused. I don't need investors. They were angry at that." Cayce hugged her before he shifted her towards the door. "Let's go speak with Joe. And we need to find something for breakfast."

"We do, but I really don't feel like anything." Haley paused in the doorway, watching Joe as he worked away preparing a meal for them all. "Joe?"

Joe looked around, a smile on his face.

"I'm sorry. I just acted like I did when Cayce was single." He stared down at the meal, a sober and sorry look on his face.

"It's perfectly fine, Joe." Haley bit at her lip before she hugged him. "I don't know how much I feel like eating, but we do need to do that." She smiled in return as he gave another sheepish grin.

Their meal finished and cleaned away, Joe sat back in his chair. He did need to speak with the couple but he wasn't sure how to do so.

"Let's spend some time in prayer, Joe." Cayce looked at his friend, his arm tightening around Haley. "We need to remind ourselves Who is in control and Who is protecting us."

Cayce raised his head after their time of prayer, refreshed to some degree. He was grateful for friends who believed and were willing to spend time with him in prayer. Cayce tilted his head to watch Haley, seeing something on her face that startled him and then worried him.

"Haley? What are you thinking?" Cayce waited somewhat impatiently for her to respond.

"I don't know what to think any more. Joe? What about that couple?" Haley turned her attention to him, feeling danger growing ever stronger around them. She prayed for safety for them and that Joe could find the people who were responsible for what they were facing.

"I don't know, Haley. I don't know much about them. They were not on our radar at all, you do know that?" Joe gave a grin at the disgruntled look on her face.

"No, I didn't know that. How would I? I didn't suspect them until Cayce started muttering in his sleep." Haley smirked at Cayce as he shook a finger at her.

"I didn't know that I suspected them, Joe. There has been nothing other than that they wanted to invest in my business. I'm not looking for any investors." Cayce thought soberly through what he had said when he didn't know that he was saying anything.

"I gather that, Cayce. Now, where do we go from here?" Joe reached for his pen and then paused, a thought gathering speed in his mind. "They wanted to invest in your company?"

Cayce nodded. He had been surprised at the time but had just set it to one side. Now, that offer seemed to be coming back to haunt him. He turned to Haley, finding her watching Joe.

"Haley? Has this happened to you?"

"What? What are you talking about?" Haley's surprised voice sounded almost too loud in the room. She winced as she turned to Cayce.

"Has anyone asked to invest in your company?" Cayce didn't think that anyone had but he wasn't sure that this hadn't happened.

Haley shook her head. She was too low-key of a business to have that happen. She was surprised that Cayce had been approached.

"No, no one has." She sighed. "Has Noah found any evidence of anyone trying to hack into our websites?" She turned as she heard a sound from Joe.

"You think someone has tried to hack into your websites? When did you contact this person?" Joe stared at them, not quite sure what to think.

"We did. It's one thing that we had to look at. Noah is a good friend and is an ethical hacker." Cayce provided the information that Joe needed. "I'll call him and ask that he speaks with you. So far, he hasn't found anything but he continues to monitor our sites."

"That's good news." Joe stared down at his notes. "Have you two received any threats by text or voice mail?" They shook their heads, causing him to sigh. "That would have been one way to try and track these people. Any strange parcels?" Again, they shook their heads.

"Where does the investigation actually stand, Joe?" Cayce reached for Haley's hand, stilling its restless motions.

"Not where we would like it. We can't confirm anyone who is after you, Haley, or your parents. The street is strangely silent about this. And that is unusual to say the least. Someone always comes forward with information." Joe turned to Haley as she made a sound.

"Someone on the police force is involved. Who are these people related to?" Haley jumped as Cayce reached to wrap her into his arms, her eyes huge as she stared at him.

"That's what we're investigating, Haley. There just seems to be someone out there who knows too much." Joe sighed as he watched the shuttered look that covered her face.

"There is?" Cayce nodded as he thought through what Joe had said. "It makes sense, doesn't it?"

"It does." Haley frowned at Joe. Then she spoke some names, causing him to stare at her in shock. "They are related to that couple."

"We didn't know that." Joe scrambled to note down the names. He didn't know how Haley was coming up with the names. "How do you know this?"

"It comes from living here all my life. People talk. You know families. Josh knows some of them which lets me know them. You'll need to speak with him." Haley stared at Joe, not sure what to say to confirm her thoughts.

"I see that, Haley. Now, Cayce? What are your feelings on what Haley has stated?" Joe waited somewhat impatiently for Cayce to respond.

Cayce rubbed at the back of his neck. He was somewhat taken aback by what she had said. He studied her with her watching him in return. He shrugged as he opened and then closed his mouth.

"I don't know what to say." Cayce's admittance finally came. "What can I say? I don't know them. I mean, I think that I have seen them around but I have had no contact with them that I know of." Joe walked away at last, not easy in his thoughts. Something was off or so it seemed with their house. He just wasn't sure what. Joe shook his head. He was sure that the house had been searched at some point. Joe was unaware that this had never happened.

Cayce stood for a moment before he headed for their work building, Haley staring after him. He shook his head before he walked around the building, searching for something that shouldn't be there. Hearing a voice behind him, Cayce turned, not surprised to see Abe and his business partner, Murphy, watching him.

"You're looking for something, Cayce?" Murphy moved away without waiting for an answer.

"Did they ever search your properties?" Abe could feel anger growing inside him.

"Not that I know of. And they should have. I would have to ask Joe." Cayce was away and running towards Murphy, Abe beside him.

"What did you find, Murphy?" Abe slid to a halt, a hand on Murphy's shoulder.

Murphy pointed, anger growing inside him, an anger that he knew that he would have to ask God for forgiveness for.

"That!" Murphy pointed to a spot high on the wall of the work building. "And you know full well there will be more planted here and on the house."

"Cameras?" Cayce swallowed hard, trying to control his emotions. "How long have they been there?"

"Likely for a while. They were probably placed before you disappeared the first time." Abe walked away, kicking angrily at a rock in his way. He spun and walked rapidly back towards the two men. "We need our team or Don's or Richard's."

Murphy held up his phone, a grim smile on his face.

"Richard's team is heading this way. Emma reached out to them, feeling the need to send them. Our guys are in training."

"That they are." Abe turned as he heard a familiar voice. "Richard? You're here with your whole team. How did you know?"

"God. And Emma. She reached out to us, asking that we appear. This is Cayce?" Richard studied the other man, seeing the stress and fear that Cayce was trying had to hide. "It's okay, Cayce. My whole team went through a tough time, just as you are. Now, what do we have here?"

"Cameras that weren't found. We don't know if a search was ever done." Abe turned as he heard a raised female voice and saw Haley standing on the back deck, waving a paper at them. "What does Haley want?"

Cayce spun and then was running towards his bride, worry uppermost in his mind. He had never heard that tone of voice from her. He could see his brothers and their wives and Josh standing behind her.

Chapter 34

Cayce wrapped Haley in his arms, knowing that she was very distraught and terrified but also angered. He had never seen her in this state. He turned to their siblings, who all shrugged, not knowing what had happened. They had just appeared as Haley pulled the sheet of paper from their mail box. None of them had had a chance to see what it said.

Abe reached carefully to take the letter from Haley's fingers, assessing her as he did so. He nodded at Murphy and Richard, who both disappeared with Richard's team of two men and two ladies, spreading out to search the property. None of them expected to find anything but they still had to search.

"Haley? What is this?" Abe's voice finally reached through Haley's terror.

"I don't know. I found it in the mail box. Who threatens us like this?" Her voice showed her outrage at the threat.

Cayce reached for the paper, reading the vile threat of harm and death to them and their families. He nodded at Abe who reached for his phone, walking away to call Joe.

Joe stared at his phone for a moment. He had not expected Abe to be reaching out to him but he was. He didn't like to hear what Abe was saying. Joe turned and trudged back to the crime scene where he was now tasked with investigating three murders. The men were rough and more than likely on the wrong side of the law. A thought paused his steps before he turned to stare behind him, feeling someone watching him. There was no way that these three murders were tied to Cayce and Haley, now was there?

Abe and Richard turned from where they had been conversing, searching for Cayce and Haley. They saw the couple with their families, worry in their demeanour. They had no idea where the couple went from there.

"Are they safe here?" Richard turned to Abe.

"I don't know, Richard. Your team's staying?"

"We are. Haley feels more comfortable with Silver and Naomi here. They need this right now." Richard nodded towards the families. "They'll want their families to stay away from them and that's just not happening."

Abe nodded in agreement, searching the area around the house.

"There are cameras here as well, Richard. Whoever put them in did a good job of hiding them."

"They did." Richard walked around the house and then the garage, frustrated at seeing the cameras. Back to stand beside Abe, he hesitated to speak. "We need to get Joe, is it, and his team out here."

"Cayce called him. Joe was on a crime scene. For now, we keep the families inside. And that is going to be difficult. Cayce said that he has a growing list of orders that he needs to work on as does Haley."

———

"They do." Richard had a thought and turned to find Joseph near him. "Joseph? What about their websites?"

"I spoke with Cayce. He has Noah trying to hack into them and watching for any activity. So far, Cayce says the sites are fine."

"At least there's that." Abe turned as he heard the back door of the house open and Cayce stepped outside to stand beside him. "Cayce?

"Abe? When can we go back to the building? We need to be working." Cayce was frustrated at not being able to do what he needed to do.

"We know that you do. Give us an hour and then we'll get you out there." Abe was stern with Cayce, knowing that he had to be. "We'll get you out there today, Cayce. Now, back inside with you."

Haley was waiting inside the door, walking into Cayce's hug. She knew their families were standing behind them but she just didn't care. Cayce tightened his arms around his bride even as his eyes closed in prayer. He was angry and he could feel the anger in Haley.

"Cayce? What are they saying?" Arlyn spoke for the other four.

"Not a lot. I suspect that there are at least cameras around our buildings. Richard and Abe are not saying." Cayce sighed. "I'm angry, people. God knows that. It's hard to acknowledge that He is in control and only wants the best for us. It's hard to be humble and accept help from others as well."

———

185

"It is, Cayce. You're not one to readily accept help, rather to be the one in the background and helping." Briar reached to lay a hand on his brother's shoulder. "We need to pray for you two and pray greatly."

"Mom and Dad? Aunt Anna? Ben? Where are they?" Cayce shared looks with his brothers and Josh.

"They're safe. Joe moved them to a safe place when Abe called him. Dad got a text message out to me but can't say where they are." Arlyn held up his phone. "It's how it has to be. He wants to send us away as well. We're not moving from here."

The three brothers nodded at each other. They had always been there for one another and had one another's back. They just didn't know when it would be over. Cayce prayed that it would be soon and that nothing worse happened to them.

"We'll pray this through, Cayce." Skylor moved to hug both Cayce and Haley before she drew Haley away with Brynne and herself. "Come with us, Haley. We'll find that prayer corner and spend the next hour in prayer. We need to do that for you."

Haley nodded soberly. She knew that she needed to pray but she wanted to stay with Cayce. She turned back to find Cayce watching her intently, nodding at her to go with his sisters-in-law.

Josh studied his sister and then her groom. He was more than a little worried about them. This adventure should never have happened but it had. All he could do was pray for them both, knowing that they were facing more than a little bit of danger.

———

Cayce turned from the other three men to stare out of the door window. He could see police officers in the yard now. This is real, he decided. Someone had been watching them far too closely. And he had to acknowledge that only God could and would be their Protector and the One who would end this, no matter how it ended.

Chapter 35

Joe walked towards Abe and Richard, knowing that they were there to provide security for the couple. He was not sure that he had made the right decision in tucking away the four older adults but he had been given little choice. His supervisor had demanded that, simply stating that they could and would be used to get to both Cayce and Haley. Josh had refused to leave, walking away from Joe and towards where Arlyn was waiting for him.

Abe turned as he heard Joe's voice and frowned. He hadn't expected Joe to appear just yet.

"Joe? You're here?"

"I am." Joe halted his forward walk, standing to watch the activities around the building. "What have you discovered, Abe? Richard? Other than the obvious."

"Emma's sending you material. You know Emma. She'll have confirmed it all. I don't know what all she's found but it's not great for Cayce or Haley." Abe rubbed at the back of his neck. He was standing facing the back of the house and saw the four men standing there, watching the activity and then focusing on the three of them.

"They're watching us, Joe." Richard gave a grim smile before he sobered. "My team is around the house, working with your force. We all want this over for the triplets. They have been through enough."

<hr>

"They have been." Joe sighed and looked up at the darkening sky. "We've had families who have faced this in more than one member. We have never had triplets before. Who is it that this person is really after?"

"Ardan. Ben. Bessie. Anna." Richard nodded as Joe shot him a quick look. "Anna. You don't know her history but those of us who do think she might be the target. Talk to her, Joe. Se has a story to tell that isn't ours to tell."

"Anna? I would never have expected that." Joe walked away as an officer approached, lost in conversation with that officer.

"She does have a story, doesn't she?" Abe sighed as well. "And I don't think the triplets know it."

"Not many do. She wouldn't have told them, not wanting them to worry excessively over her. It's who she is." Richard pointed back at the house. "We need to go and speak with them. But what do we tell them? We haven't been told much."

"No, we haven't been told much. Murphy? You've spoken with Emma?" Abe waited for Murphy to speak.

"I have been. We need to speak with all of them in the house and then move them somewhere that's safer than this. Emma suggested our compound but they won't go for it." Murphy gave a quick grin. "Ian has offered to fly them somewhere they would be safe."

Abe grinned as well before he sobered. Ian was known to offer that to the ladies in distress. Abe's team always teased him about that but stood behind him when he offered it.

"He would do that. For now, let's make some plans. We need to hide them away." Richard walked away, heading for his team.

Abe nodded in agreement. He just didn't know where to put them.

"They won't leave, Abe. You know that as well as I do. Don's offered to move his team in as well." Don was another friend with a security team of six.

"We might need that. For now, we'll see what they have to say." Abe walked towards the house, finding the four men walking towards him. "Guys?"

"Abe? What is consensus? Where do you plan on putting us?" Cayce gave a grim smile, bringing smiles to the others' faces.

"Right at the moment? We're not putting you anywhere. You won't go and your ladies won't." Abe turned for a moment, studying the sky or what he could see of it for the twilight. "We'll keep you all here for tonight and then reassess in the morning."

"That sounds like a plan." Briar and Josh walked back up the steps after Briar had commented on Abe's statement. This was not what Abe or Murphy had expected.

Arlyn stared after the two, waiting for Cayce to react.

"What all is out there, Abe?" Cayce's voice had a bite to it, something unusual for him.

"Cameras, Cayce. Many cameras. You didn't know?" Abe watched Cayce closely, trying to assess him. That was impossible for him to do.

"No. If I had, they would have been gone." He gave Abe and then Murphy a hard stare. "That's why we haven't been receiving the packages, the text messages, the voice mails. They are following us, we know that. We've seen them but not close enough to be sure of who they are. What else can we say?" Cayce spun on his heel, walking rapidly back to the house where Haley was waiting for him. He just wrapped her into his arms and then turned her back to the house.

"He's hurting, Abe." Arlyn watched his brother. He was angry that Cayce had to face what he and Briar had. He prayed hard for his brother, begging God's to protect the couple.

"He is. We all know to some extent how he and Haley are feeling. You know our stories." Murphy walked away towards where Richard was waiting for him.

"He's right, guys." Abe drew in a deep breath. "The techs will be a while. I know that you aren't hungry but we need to remember to eat." Abe turned the two back towards the house, following them despite being lost in thought.

Haley was waiting for Abe, a shuttered look on her face. She simply handed him her phone and walked away. She knew full well that he would take it to Joe. Haley didn't want to be the one who did that.

Abe studied her phone before handing it over to Murphy who handed it over to Richard. The three men shared looks. The text messages were finally starting, letting them know that whoever it was knew that their cameras and whatnot had been found. They were watching the couple that closely.

"Do we even have a sense of who it is or why?" Murphy paced around the two other men, deep in thought.

"No, we don't, I don't think." Abe spun to stare at Joe. "Joe may have an idea. And Emma has been trying to reach us." Abe reached for his phone, speaking with his wife who had tracked down information that no one else had been able to find. He pocketed his phone thoughtfully, not speaking for a moment.

Murphy studied him before he turned to Richard who simply shrugged. They watched as the seven people from the house approached them and then surrounded them, Richard's team standing with their backs to the group and watching the activity around them.

Chapter 36

Haley ran for the house two days later, hearing the crunching of the gravel from the driveway behind her. She slammed open the door and then slammed it shut, locking it and then running for the office. Her phone had been left there. She needed to find Cayce who was away from the house at the moment. Haley just couldn't remember why.

Hearing the hammering at the doors, Haley reached for her phone, frantically dialling for help. Her voice was almost too low for the dispatch operator to hear. Her phone was dropped on the desk without disconnecting the call. Haley searched for somewhere to hide, not finding it.

The sound of the back door crashing open had her stifling a scream. She couldn't find anywhere to hide. Her phone was tucked into her jeans pocket even as she spun to face the men who appeared in front of her. Haley backed away, heading for the French doors in the office.

"What do you want?" Her voice was high-pitched as her fear came through. She felt the door behind her and wrenched at the lock before she had the door open and was running through it, the door slamming behind her. Searching desperately for a place to hide, Haley screamed as she ran into a body. She struggled to escape the hands that reached for her and then she was running with the man, feeling safe.

Richard and Naomi had appeared just as the men broke into the house. Naomi had headed for the house to watch quietly as the men ran back out of the house through the French door. Richard simply reached for Haley and ran with her, searching as well for a hiding place. Seeing the pile of stacked wood, Richard shoved Haley behind it before he crouched in front of her, his weapon in his hand. He could feel Haley's hand shoving at him but he refused to move.

Sirens broke through the morning air and emergency lights lit up the sky as the police arrived, sent by the dispatcher. The officers scattered, finding the men spinning to face them before trying to run. Naomi waited patiently near the house, simply giving her statement as to what she found.

Richard drew in a deep breath before he was on his feet, finding Joe walking his way. Naomi had sent him that way. He stood in such a way that he could watch Haley who was on her feet and angry as well as terrified. It had been just too close for her, Richard knew. He had no idea how she had managed to escape the men but God had put Naomi and himself there at the right time.

"Richard?" Joe kept his voice low even as he stepped to where he could watch Haley. He found her glaring at him, anger sparking from her eyes.

"We were here in time, Joe. They meant to take her." Richard rubbed at his face, not sure what to say. "I found Haley running from the house. Naomi stayed near the back door. They broke in through that. Haley should be able to tell you what happened before we arrived." Richard gave a quick grin at Haley as she stared at him, mouth open before she snapped it closed.

"Haley? We'll keep you here for now." Joe shrugged out of his jacket and wrapped it around her shoulders, seeing her hands clutching at it. He frowned as he saw how shaky her hands were. "Talk to me, Haley. What happened? And where is Cayce?"

"Cayce had an appointment this morning that would take a few hours." Haley leaned against the pile of firewood, her legs not quite steady enough to hold her upright. "Joe? Who are they?"

Joe turned to look towards the house, seeing that the men had been removed.

"Someone after you?" He gave a quick grin as her glare turned to him once more. "They were determined to take you away from your home, Haley. An investigator will be speaking with them. It won't be me. Now, talk to me. Tell me what happened."

Haley shook her head, breaking away from Richard and Joe and running towards where Naomi was waiting for her. Naomi lifted a hand to Richard and then with an arm around Haley, directed her around the house to Richard's vehicle and tucked her inside. Naomi then stood, watching the neighbours who had gathered outside as the activity continued around the house.

Haley sighed, knowing that she had to speak with Joe, but wanting Cayce there when she did. That wouldn't happen, she knew. Joe would track her down and force her to talk. Only she didn't know what she could tell him. Her eyes found the sky and she began to beg God for this to be over. Haley wanted to go on with her life with Cayce and that couldn't happen while they were under attack. And that was exactly what it was.

"Naomi? What would you do?" Haley finally spoke, her eyes on Joe as he approached her.

"Talk to Joe first. Then find my hubby." Naomi grinned at her. "Our team went through adventures like this. It was tough. But we knew that God was there and in control. He only wants the best for you. That's a given. It is Who God is and Who He wants to be in your life. He has already walked this path before you and knows exactly what you are facing and how you are reacting. Keep your hand in His, Haley. He will never leave you or forsake you. He has brought you and Cayce together in His plans for your lives. Trust Him, no matter how hard it is."

Haley had focused on Naomi as she was speaking, feeling the ice around her heart that had developed during the adventure that she and Cayce were involved in breaking to pieces. She sniffed as she tried to control her tears.

"Thank you, Naomi. Your words make complete sense." Haley reached to hug her friend. "We need to get together with your team and your spouses when this is all over." She looked past Naomi towards Joe. "Joe? You need to know what happened, don't you? I don't know those men. I just heard them running towards me and hid in the office. When they appeared in the office doorway, I backed up to the French doors. I hadn't locked them again this morning. God must have done that. I ran and that's when Richard found me. I don't know anything more than that."

———

Joe had already gathered that was what had happened, given what the officers had found and what Richard had advised him. He shook his head. Haley should have been taken from her house and hadn't been. That made him wonder if that had been the real reason for this.

"Were they after me, Joe, or after Cayce?" Haley's question echoed his thoughts.

Joe stared at her, not sure what she meant but God did. Of that, he was totally convinced. He felt the hand of God in the situation. Turning, he watched as Cayce ran towards Haley, finding Haley leaping from Richard's truck and into Cayce's arms.

Chapter 37

Holding his bride tight in his arms, Cayce stared down at Haley and then at their home. He didn't know what the activity was for or for how long it had been going on. Haley had been safe when he drove away from their home a couple of hours ago. Cayce had been shocked to receive that call from Joe, simply asking if he could return to their home. Haley needed him. He had not hesitated to leave where he was, excusing himself from the Bible study.

"Joe? What is going on? What happened?" Cayce bit out his words, knowing that he would need to ask forgiveness for them.

"What happened? Let's just say that Haley was chased into your home and then escaped the men chasing her through the French doors of your office. Richard hid her. Now, we'll need to walk through your home. And you won't be staying here for the foreseeable future." Joe waited for Cayce to maneuver Haley towards the house, not disturbed at how reluctant that she was to move there.

"Haley?" Cayce waited for her to speak but she didn't, simply shaking her head. She just couldn't tell him how fearful she was or what the men had been shouting. She had not even told Joe. "Let's go, sweetheart. We'll walk through the house, pack some belongings and then move somewhere for the duration."

Haley was shaking her head.

———

"I'm not leaving our home, Cayce. They'll just follow us. Here? We know the house and know how to escape or hide. We don't have that information somewhere else." Haley looked up at him, seeing his understanding on his face.

"I understand, sweetheart. We'll stay." Cayce reached for her hand, leading her through the house. "We'll find someone to replace the door."

Joe watched them before he shook his head. It was what he expected them to do. He just didn't want them to do that. He could feel the danger that they were facing closing in on them and he had no way to stop it.

"Cayce? What can we do to make it safer for you two?" Joe walked back through the house, assessing it from a security standpoint.

"I don't know, Joe. You can't move in here nor can anyone else." Cayce hugged Haley tighter. "We'll pray for protection. God will protect us and only allow what He wills for us."

Haley turned in his arms to face Joe and then looked past him at Richard and Naomi. She was terrified, she had to admit to herself, but she was also determined not to run from their enemy any more.

"We're not running, Joe. Not any more. We'll face them here." Haley bit at her lip. "What do you know that you can tell us?"

"What can I tell you? Not a lot. We just don't have the names for those behind it all. The men and women, yes women, who we have arrested are not saying anything. That is either because of fear or because they really don't know."

"I would certainly think that it's because of fear. If they are scaring us this much, how much are they scaring some of them?" Haley didn't expect an answer from Joe. "I mean, there are some who won't scare. We all know that. But how do we draw out the ones behind it all? Until we do that, we can't truly live." Haley felt Cayce's arms tighten around her. "So, once more, Joe, how do we do this?"

"I don't know, to tell you the truth, Haley. I don't know how to keep you safe. You're not getting all the threats that people usually get. That tells me that someone is close to you and knows exactly what you're doing." Joe's hand went up at their protest. "We need a complete list of your friends and any relatives that you have not given us." Joe reached for the papers that Cayce pulled from his jacket pocket. "Prepared were you, Cayce?"

"We thought about this last night, Joe. We want this over, as Haley has stated. Will this do it?" Cayce didn't back down from his friend.

Joe studied the names, a finger tapping at one.

"This one? This couple? Why would you put them down? I didn't know that you were friends with them."

Cayce peered at the paper as did Haley. They shared a look before both nodded.

"Them. We don't know them other than seeing them around town and at craft shows. They always seem to be so interested in various arts and crafts. But the consensus among the artists is that they are not on the up and up. They have crossed over many times into criminal activities. Only no one has been able to prove that. That's what we want you to do. I heard from Emma. She's finding information on that couple and will forward it to you once she has confirmed it. Apparently, their reach is also to many towns and many forces are investigating them. It had to be us, didn't it?" Cayce's voice was grim as he spoke.

"It did have to be someone, Cayce." Haley leaned against him, drawing from his strength. "God knows what He is doing by choosing us to do that. I just wish He had chosen someone else."

Joe gave a brief grin as he heard Richard and Naomi behind him and heard their comments that God had chosen them as well.

"He does that, Haley." Richard bit at his lip for a moment, not sure how to put into words his thoughts.

"He does, Richard." Cayce studied his kitchen, watching as a renovator was replacing the broken-in door. "We'll be as safe here as we would anywhere else. Go home, Richard and Naomi. Spend time with your families. That's what we want."

Richard and Naomi finally nodded before they walked away. They knew that their team would be back around the next day as would Abe's team and also their friend, Don's. They had to respect the wishes of the couple. They would just be around and out of sight, providing the protection that was needed.

Joe walked away at last, heading for his office and the work that was piling up. He studied his phone, a sigh rising within him. There just wasn't enough time in the day, he decided, knowing that he had more urgent investigations at present. He had to set this one aside.

Chapter 38

The next morning, Cayce carefully and thoughtfully walked around the house and then the work building. He didn't see that anything had been replaced but then he wasn't trained in that field. He knew that Richard or Don or Abe would be around, staying in the shadows as much as they could.

Haley watched him before she turned to study the back deck. Something was off there but she had no idea what. She sighed, something she seemed to be doing a lot. Cayce watched her from the bottom of the steps before he too studied the back deck.

"Something is off, isn't it?" Cayce's voice sounded too loud in the early morning air and he winced.

Haley nodded, knowing that he was picking up something as well. She just wasn't seeing what it was.

"There is, Cayce, but what? Do you see anything off? You're more familiar with the deck than I am." Haley leaned against him, knowing that he would see something and then tell her.

"There is something off, but I don't know what." Cayce paced the deck, studying everything that he could. "I just don't see anything."

"They're playing mind games with us. Our security feed is down as well." Haley yanked open the back door and disappeared, leaving Cayce to stare after her before he followed her.

"It is? When?" Cayce reached for the tablet on the counter, pulling up the security system. "It says it went off line about two this morning. I didn't hear anything outside."

"Nor did I." Haley poured their mugs of coffee, almost too full before she turned to Cayce, tears clouding her eyes. "What do we do now? We have to end this."

"We do." Cayce reached for her hand as they sat, his head bowing in prayer. He was begging God, he knew, to end this that day. He was suddenly and deeply afraid. Cayce raised his head to study his bride, fearful that he would lose her.

Haley reached for a pad of paper and pen, looking at the notes that they had made. She sighed to herself before her prayers echoed Cayce's, begging God to protect him.

"Do we start putting our plans into effect?" Haley waited almost impatiently for Cayce to respond.

"We do. Starting today." Cayce was on his feet, preparing a quick breakfast for them. "Do you need to be in your shop today?"

"I should be but I updated our web sites to state that due to unforeseen circumstances, orders will be delayed." Haley reached for a piece of toast. "I think that should work. We can get caught up quickly, I think. Skylor and Brynne had offered to sort out the orders and do the making for us once we're through this."

"They will do that. It's part of who they are as people but it's also family." Cayce sat for a moment, not sure how to continue. "I love you so much, sweetheart. I am so afraid that I'll lose you."

Haley reached to hug him, not hearing anything outside.

"I love you too and that's my fear, that I'll lose you." Haley was on her feet, heading for the front door.

Cayce stared after her before he followed her, not sure what she was planning.

"Haley? Sweetheart? What are you thinking?" Cayce waited on the steps to the front porch as she studied the gardens and then the facade of the house.

"I don't know other than I want this over with." Haley spun in a circle, thinking that she was being watched but not seeing anyone. "Someone is watching us, Cayce."

"They will be, sweetheart. We just don't know where they are or when they will attack us again." Cayce moved to stop Haley's movements. "We need to keep praying, sweetheart. God is in control, we know that. We just don't know who or why."

"We do know that, Cayce. I just want this over and I don't know that it will be." Haley spun as she heard a slight noise and then reached for Cayce's hand to pull him back into the house. "Someone is close to us."

Cayce locked the door and then stood and watched the three men who appeared on the city sidewalk, their attention on the house.

"There are three of them out there." Cayce hugged Haley to him. "I want to go out but I don't know that it's safe."

Haley snorted, bringing a quick smile to Cayce's face.

"Let's just go. Your truck is in the garage and we can just drive away." Haley spun, reaching for her jacket and purse, and then handing Cayce his jacket.

"Are you sure?" Cayce was sure of what they were needing to do.

"I am. We need to take back our lives and this is part of how we do that." Haley opened the truck door and hopped in, fastening her seat belt and then staring at Cayce, who stood, shocked at her quick movements. "Well? What are you waiting for?"

Cayce stared at her for a moment before he grinned and then jumped behind the wheel. The garage door opened behind his truck and he hit the gas to shoot out of it. A simple click of the opener closed the door as Cayce hit the street and then drove off.

Haley watched behind them, seeing the men scattering to their vehicles and then pursuing them.

"They are following us, Cayce. What is your plan?" Haley continued to watch the vehicles behind them even as Cayce watched around and ahead of them.

Cayce shot her a startled look before he gave a quick grin.

"My plan? I thought that you had a plan."

"We'll come up with a plan but where are you heading?" Haley shot him a quick look as well before she turned back to watch the men.

"I have no idea. Any thoughts?"

"Yes, the library. We have research to do, don't we?" Haley gave a smirk. "They'll just have to come in and read or wait outside."

Chapter 39

Cayce slowed to a stop in a deserted area of town but it was not his choice to do so. The vehicles had surrounded his truck and stopped him. He reached to ensure that the doors were locked before he reached for Haley's hand. He could hear her audible prayers as she begged God to save them before she began to pray all the verses that she could think of. A grim smile crossed his face as he tightened his hand on hers. Cayce feared for their lives as the men approached the truck and began to hammer at the windows.

Haley's head was turning as she searched for a way to escape. She couldn't see one at the present time.

"What if they break the windows, Cayce? What do we do?" Haley's voice quivered with the fear, no terror, that she was trying hard to hide.

"We'll escape, sweetheart." Cayce studied the men, recognizing them as other crafters. "What is going on? These men are fellow crafters."

Haley peered at them, frowning at them before she nodded.

"They are. So, if they are fellow crafters, who is behind them? They belong to a cooperative for their crafts, don't they?"

"They do. And that explains why we haven't been receiving all those things that people under attack usually do. They've been able to stay that close to us."

Haley's phone was out as she sent off a text message to Joe. "I've let Joe know where we are and who's here." Haley peered at her phone screen, a hand cupped around it to block the sunshine. "Joe's on his way. He's sending patrol vehicles for now."

Cayce looked around as he heard the sounds of sirens. The men spun and ran for their vehicles, not making it away in time before the patrol vehicles surrounded them.

Watching the activity outside of their truck, Cayce and Haley sat silent, not sure what they should be do. Obviously, they weren't going anywhere any time soon.

Joe spoke with the patrol officers, his eyes on the men who were now handcuffed and sitting in the back of the vehicles. He looked over at the truck before he shook his head at something that was said to him.

Walking towards the truck, Joe watched as Cayce rolled down his window. Haley was leaning against Cayce, watching in turn as Joe approached them. Joe stopped and leaned against the side of the truck, staring ahead of him. He really didn't know what to say to the couple or how to approach what he needed to.

"Joe? Do you know who they are?" Haley's voice held her anger.

"No. How be you tell me?" Joe finally looked at her, drawing in a quick breath at the look on her face.

"They are members of a craft cooperative. We don't do the same items but we know them from craft shows and groups." Haley blew out a deep breath. "Look for whoever it is that is behind the co-op. That will give you who you are looking for." She sat back, turning to look out of the side window.

Joe stared at her for a moment before he looked at Cayce, who just shrugged.

"She's right, Joe. They are crafters. We don't know them well. Something about them kept us separate from them. When can we leave?" Cayce was getting tired of being blocked in. His phone had also been vibrating almost incessantly and he knew that it would be his family or Haley's family looking for them.

"Soon. We're having tow trucks come and take their cars. Tell me what happened."

"What happened?" Cayce began to shake his head. "We were at home, saw them on the sidewalk, and just decided to leave. We drove away and they followed before they blocked us in. Haley called you once that happened." He knew that Haley had turned to watch them.

Finally able to drive away, Cayce headed for a nearby coffee shop, going through the drive-through and accepting the cardboard tray with their drinks. He pulled into a parking spot before he reached for Haley, hugging her tight to him.

"You're okay?" His voice was low.

"I think I am at last. How are you?" Haley hugged him, not wanting to let go. Her fear was finally dropping in intensity.

"I'm okay if you're okay." Cayce bit at his lip. "This is where we have to be very careful. It will take a day or so, I suspect, to arrest the ones responsible for all this."

"It will. But God will be there for us. He has brought us through so far and will continue to do so." Haley swiped at the tears on her face. She didn't apologize for crying. Cayce just reached out a handkerchief to help wipe her face dry.

"He has, sweetheart. He has done that. It has taught me that being humble and waiting on him, while very hard, is what we have to do. We reach out and help others. It's hard to step back and accept help."

"It is, but it's what we need to do in certain circumstances." Haley looked up at him. "I love you, Cayce. God has given me just who I need in my life."

"And I love you too. You are the lady I had dreamt about for years but despaired of finding." His words stopped as images suddenly clarified in his mind. "I know who it is, sweetheart. I remember what happened to me." His head dropped against the steering wheel as he felt Haley's arms come around him and he heard the prayer that she was whispering. "It's not the co-op, Haley."

"It's not? Then who is it?" Haley waited impatiently for him to raise his head. She could feel the shudders running through his body. "Cayce? Sweetheart? Who is it?" Haley drew in a deep breath as Cayce raised his head and she saw the devastation on it. "Cayce?"

———

"Haley? How do I say who it is? No one will believe me." Cayce reached to hug her, not wanting to state the name but knowing that he needed to.

"Who is it, Cayce? I can't tell you who to talk to unless you tell me." Haley's eyes grew huge and her mouth opened and closed as Cayce said the name. "It can't be!"

Cayce too looked devastated as he leaned back to look at Haley.

"It's him, Haley. We need to prove it. I just don't know if we can."

Chapter 40

Papers seemed to be scattered over every surface in their home office. The families were all there, including the parents and Anna. The four older adults had just refused to stay away when Ardan had spoken with Cayce earlier that day. The conversation was quiet for the most part but becoming heated as one of the younger men tried to make their point.

Cayce sat back for a moment, exhausted and then glanced at his clock. It was after three in the morning. He rose and stretched, walking away from his desk. Arlyn and Briar stood as well, following their brother. Cayce stopped in the kitchen doorway and watched as Bessie and Anna worked away, preparing more food for them.

"Mom?" Cayce waited for his mother to turn to him. "Are we on the right track? I think that we are. Emma's been sending all sorts of information as well confirming this."

Bessie's hands stilled before she reached for a towel to dry them, turning to face her three sons. She stopped for a moment to study them, wondering when they grew up and became men. It seemed like only yesterday that she and Ardan were struggling to manage the newborn triplets.

"I think that you are, son. You know, he's changed over the last few years. He's not the same as he was when he came to our church in the start of his ministry." Bessie reached to hug each of her sons, holding onto Cayce just that little bit longer. He had been the quieter one of the three, seeming to need her just that little bit more than his brothers. "Is that what you've been picking up in the last couple of years? You have not been comfortable with him for years."

"No, I haven't been, Mom. I just didn't know why. I thought it was wrong of me to feel that way." Cayce bit at his lip, his eyes on Haley as she was nodding. "Haley?"

"I have never really liked him. I just didn't know why. He talked good but his walk didn't always seem to follow that talk." Haley sighed, a deep up from the toes sigh. "I would see him in places that he shouldn't be. I never really analyzed why I felt that way."

"God kept us safe." Cayce reached for Haley, wrapping her into his arms. "He does that to protect us. We sometimes get feelings about someone or sense that something is off with them."

"He does, son." Ardan had come to find the three boys as he called them. "Now, what do we do with this information? How much do we pass onto Joe?"

"None at the moment." Cayce shook his head at his father's words. "Samuel said that he, Blackie, and Simon are heading this way today." He looked towards the door as he heard a light tap at it. "Who's here at this time of the morning?"

Anna returned to the kitchen followed by the three men Cayce had just mentioned.

"You're here?" Cayce reached to shake their hands.

"We are. We have word that your antagonist is heading this way and now." Samuel's voice was grim as was his face. "We need to come up with some plans to protect you two. He means to kill you both."

Cayce's face paled as did Haley's. His arms tightened on his bride before he nodded.

"Of course. His heart is black, isn't it?" Haley was angry and wasn't ready to ask for forgiveness for that. "He's after Cayce because Cayce is humble and seeks the best for others and not for himself. That man only wants what is good for him. I've seen that particularly in the last few years."

"That is true, Haley." Simon studied her, a frown on his face. "But why is he after you?"

"I can tell you why." Josh waved a piece of paper in the air. "This is what he's after you for, Haley." He soberly handed it over to her, not wanting to but also knowing that she needed to understand why.

Haley stared at the paper, shock on her face. She looked up at her brother.

"This? This goes back to when I was a teen. I didn't date his son?" Haley leaned back against Cayce. "It goes back to that? I never knew his son. I have never seen him. In fact, I never knew that he had a son. Did anyone else?"

They were all shaking their heads. None of them were aware that their minister had a wife, let alone a son. He had kept it well hidden.

"So, how do we do this then?" Cayce hugged Haley tighter. "We need to plan now that we know this."

"His son is dead, Cayce." Arlyn looked up. "Emma just sent information that confirms he has a son, illegitimate at that. He has never married." He looked around at the ones in the kitchen. "She also says that he has been going to the streets here to find someone to take out Cayce and Haley. He has had no takers, so she thinks he'll try it himself."

"And that makes it so dangerous." Briar rubbed at the side of his head, a headache beginning. "How do we do this and keep you two safe?"

Simon held out a paper bag.

"These are wired transmitters that we want Cayce and Haley to wear. I suggest that we confront him at the church. There will be little danger to others and we will make sure that we are close by." Simon had discussed this with Abe, Samuel, and Blackie. This had been their consensus of how to proceed.

The group finally settled on a plan. Before they walked out of the house to put it into place, they arranged themselves into a circle. With arms around one another, one after the other prayed, begging God for protection on the couple, knowing full well that this was an extremely dangerous and possible life-ending process that they were heading out of the house to put into place.

Haley stood for a moment in the master bedroom, her eyes on the mirror above the dresser. Her face was white and tired, dark circles under her eyes.

She wanted this over and over that day. Cayce came to find her and simply wrapped her into his arms before he kissed her and then reached for their jackets. The wires that Samuel had prepared for them were on their bodies and working.

"All set?" Cayce kept his voice just loud enough for Haley to hear.

"I guess. Are we doing the right thing, Cayce?" Haley stared up at his beloved face, scared that their actions that day would result in her losing him.

Chapter 41

Cayce carefully shut the truck door before he walked around to help Haley down from the vehicle. He wrapped her into a hug before he stood and looked towards the church. His hand tightened on Haley's before they shared a look and then walked towards the building, knowing that their enemy was there. They walked forward in confidence that God was with them and walking ahead of him. They had both nodded when Blackie had reminded them that God had walked this path for them many years ago and that He alone was in control of what happened.

"Where is he?" Haley's voice was barely audible.

"He's here somewhere. I can feel the evil around us." Cayce's steps paused for a moment before he looked towards the cemetery. "That way, I think, Haley."

"The cemetery? Really?" Haley sighed. "I guess you're right. It's kind of ironic, isn't it? God is here, isn't He?"

"He is." Cayce was nodding. "He is, sweetheart. We know that even though we can't see Him." He was watching Haley's face and saw the moment that it became shuttered and fear lurked even deeper in her eyes. "Haley?"

"Cayce? He's here. On the other side. Oh, no! He's coming towards us." Haley tried to move backwards but felt something hit her back.

A man had appeared behind them. Cayce and Haley could hear the chatter from those who were watching, warning them. Cayce tightened his hold on Haley's hand as he stood, feet spread shoulder width apart, ready to face the antagonist.

"Well, Jim Laney. What have you to say for yourself?" Haley went on the offensive, not quite what they had planned. She could hear the muttering from those listening. She didn't care. She wanted this over today and now.

" Haley. Haley. Haley. What do you have to say for yourself?" Jim Laney walked towards them, not the man who he had been portraying for so many years. The evil that was in his soul had become evident on his face and in his voice.

"I haven't done anything, Jim. It's you who has. Why?" Haley shifted closer to Cayce, her eyes raising briefly to see Simon and Blackie moving in behind Jim. She drew in a deep breath. Joe was with them.

"Why? Because I could. Because I wanted to. Your family has been too goody-goody. You refused to date my son." Jim stopped short of them, a smirk on his face. "But your life stops here. It is fitting that we meet in a cemetery."

"Really? Fitting?" Cayce spoke at last. "I don't think that it will end here, Jim. And I want to know why me."

"Why you? You're a goody two-shoes as well." Jim didn't mince his words. "You pretend to be so humble but you're not. You brag about what you do."

Cayce was shaking his head, knowing that what Jim was spouting off was totally incorrect and not him.

"I have never bragged about anything, Jim. You know that. Now that man behind us? Your son? The one who pretended to be dead? He has always bragged about whatever it was that he did. You did as well. You are projecting yourselves and your actions onto me. You know that full well." Cayce threw himself to his left, tugging Haley with her. Her scream split the area, followed by yells and shouts from their three friends and then the officers who had also surrounded them.

Simon and Blackie reached for the couple, dragging them to their feet, and then running with them away from the scene. The shouts and yells to surrender continued before Jim and his son, Tom, surrendered. They had no choice.

Simon stared at the scene, having tucked Cayce and Haley away in a vehicle. Not their own, he had decided. They needed it gone over by the crime scene techs. He felt something was off about it.

Cayce shoved open the truck door and then slid out of it to stand beside Simon. He too watched the activity where they had just stood, his face pale with shock. He could feel Haley's arms around his neck as she watched as well.

"Simon? Is it over?" Cayce was reluctant to even ask.

"It is, Cayce. I do believe it is. Joe will be speaking with you later today." Simon turned, feeling relief course through him. "Back in the truck, Cayce. Let us drive you home."

Late that evening, Cayce walked through the house looking for Haley. He found her in the office, curled up in an upholstered chair, a sober look on her face. He scooped her into his arms and sat back down, holding her tight. He could feel the sobs that she was trying hard not to shed.

"Okay, sweetheart?" Cayce finally spoke, a kiss dropped on her head.

"I'll get there, just as you will. Did he really think that would harm us?" Haley looked up at Cayce, seeing him shaking his head.

"He did. That's how depraved that he was. The church will need to do a lot of healing to recover from years of this man. He talked in the correct manner."

"But there was always something that kept anyone from getting close to him. Now we know." Haley snuggled down against Cayce as her eyes closed and she slept, the worry and stress of the past few months releasing.

Cayce's head rested against his beloved Haley before he too slept. God had been gracious and good, he decided, sending prayers of praise up to his Heavenly Father.

A year later, Ardan stood with his arm around Bessie, his eyes on his family. He could see the three boys huddled with Josh before tossing around a football in their backyard. The ladies were with Anna, who held Arlyn's young son. Briar's young daughter, just a few weeks old, was in her mother's arms as the ladies laughed. He smiled slightly as he studied Haley, knowing that their third grandchild would be with the family in just a few weeks. Ardan was happy and content.

"I am so glad their adventures are over, Ardan." Bessie reached to hug her husband. "I was so afraid that we would lose one of them."

"As was I. God has protected us greatly over the last months with what they went through and then through the trials." Ardan paused for a moment, his eyes on Anna. Something seemed off about her that day and he just didn't know what. "There's something going on with Anna."

"There is." Bessie nodded. "She won't tell us, though."

"No, she won't." Ardan watched as Bessie headed for their boys, Ben taking her spot beside him.

Late that night, Cayce turned to find Haley wrapping her arms around him. He kissed her and then just held her.

"Okay, sweetheart?" He could tell that she was uncomfortable.

"I'm okay. This child is what the problem is. He or she is very active today. I think they're wanting to start playing with their cousins." She smirked at him.

Cayce began to laugh as his hand landed on her abdomen, feeling their child moving.

"The next few weeks will drag and fly." He looked at Haley. "Have I told you today how much I love you?"

"You have. And I love you too." Haley's head rested against his shoulder. "I was so afraid, love, that we would lose each other or one of our families."

"Me, too." Cayce shifted to a more comfortable position. "Jim and his son hid their secret lives well. I never expected that he was behind a lot of crime with the youth."

"No one did, I don't think. It is a relief for the town to have answers that were never available before. Joe touched base a while ago, just to ensure that we are okay. He felt bad that it took so long to find the man."

"Joe shouldn't feel like that. It wasn't his fault. It was the depravity of the man and his son. It's the church who really needs to heal. No one seems to blame us, but I sometimes wonder if there are some that do."

Haley drew in a deep breath. "I love you, Cayce."

"I love you too, Haley." He kissed her before he hugged her tighter. "My life would be so empty without you."

———

"Was that really what it was all about? Jealousy?" Haley didn't think that it was but she had to ask.

"From what we learned in court and from Joe, it was. Jim had a sick, twisted mind. He hurt so many people in the years that he was here. We're not the only ones that he tried this with but thank God that we were the last." Cayce grew silent. He could only praise God that he had protected his beloved Haley and himself and their families. So much could have gone wrong except for God intervening.

"God was good, Cayce. He proved once more that He is our precious Abba Father, wanting only the best for us and now for our family." Haley's eyes closed as she slept, content in her love for Cayce and his for her and now with their family growing, she knew that God had truly blessed them.

Cayce thought back to when it all happened. Laney had confessed to kidnapping him and then leaving him to die somewhere. He was not to have survived, that much he knew. He just wasn't sure how he had escaped from Laney and then found his way to Haley. No one could explain that.

Dear Readers:

Thank you once more for picking up one of my stories and reading it. This novel ends the trilogy of the Koyle triplets. It was something different to write about triplets rather than just siblings. A challenge for sure.

God is there for each one of us, no matter what we face. He is our loving Abba Father who wants only the best for His children. We walk away from Him but He never leaves us. It is with confidence that we can say that He has walked our path before us and with us.

As always, characters from other novels walk into the story. Abe and Emma and their team are from *His Guardians*. Noah is from *His Warriors*. Blackie and Simon are from *Mistletoe Treasures*. My characters just can't stay in their own stories.

During the writing of this novel (which took much longer than I planned), I began the process of repainting my home. The colours in Cayce's kitchen? Those are the colours in mine. It feels like spring with the fresh paint.

It was also with sadness that the week that I finished this book also brought devastation to my life. Both of Shelties became ill and I had to let them go. Liam was 14 and Natalie almost 13. It has left huge holes in my life. God is with me as I walk this path with just my tuxedo and calico cats.

May God richly bless you as you walk with Him and follow His leading.

Ronna